Stealing the Magic

The Story of a Caged Magician

Tony Myers

 www.trafford.com
North America & international
toll-free: 1 888 232 4444 (USA & Canada)
fax: 812 355 4082

Acknowledgments

———— ∿∿◦◦⊙⊙↞⊙↞⊙◦◦∿∿ ————

I WANT TO SHOW MY GRATITUDE to a number of people who made this book possible. Without them, this book would not be what it is today. Thank you guys! I appreciate all you have done.

I would like to start by saying thank you to all the fans of my first book, *Singleton*. Your emails and notes were very encouraging and helped to push me to write another book. Thank you for all of your support of the book.

Dave and Karen Wilson also receive a large amount of my gratitude. Dave, thank you for your encouragement and support of me as an author. I also consider it a great privilege to call you friend. Karen, thank you for your editing services. I know you spent many hours on the manuscript and for that I am extremely grateful. You are one very talented editor. Keep up the good work!

I also want to say thank you to my late grandfather, Ron Duranske. He was a talented magician, and he always seemed to have a new trick up his sleeve. Thank you for using your talents and tricks, not for your own fame or pride, but simply to entertain us as grandkids. You are greatly missed, but your legacy lives on.

Where would I be without my family? I want to thank both my immediate and extended family. Y'all were inspiring and encouraging. I appreciate all the excitement and interest in this book, as well as for *Singleton*. I especially want to mention Charity, Hannah Beth, and Anthony. I love you guys so much! I also look forward to meeting our new little guy who will be here by the time this book is published. I already love you, Little Man.

Lastly, I would like to give my love and gratitude to God. Every good and perfect gift comes from You. Thank you for sending your Son to die on the cross for my sins. He is the greatest gift ever given. To Him be all glory, honor, and praise!

To all my youth kids,
Stay on the Straight and Narrow,
and don't steal magic.

❖

Prologue

CHARLES CHESTERTON STARED OUT THE window of his second story office, looking out onto the city of Reno. The traffic was streaming by at a reasonable pace. It was a cloudy day in March. He had another performance coming up that evening. The pace was grueling.

He focused on his reflection in the window. He was already in his tuxedo as he had afternoon rehearsals coming up soon. His hair was a mess, and there were large bags under his eyes. He looked like a worn out, middle-aged magician who could use some time away from the stage.

He walked over to his desk and poured himself a small taste of scotch. Needing to relax, he sat in his desk chair. The phone had been ringing off the hook this morning. It was a busy week and he was thankful for the few minutes of silence.

He had been performing as a headlining magician for the last year and had built a fair amount of credibility in the area.

Many of his tricks were original and other magicians weren't able to duplicate his methods, even when they knew his secrets. At his current pace Charles Chesterton would rise to complete stardom by the end of the following year. His wealth was growing substantially, and his theater had even rewarded him with his own office and manager. He was the envy of many young magicians and street performers. Life seemed to be going well.

But none of this mattered to him. The clouds outside his window were symbolic of how he felt. None of the accolades had brought him the satisfaction he so greatly desired. Sure, he found enjoyment and pleasure in all of his stardom, but it was not what he wanted. The magic was what he truly loved, and he wanted more. He wanted to feel the rush of a new trick. To have a new secret and to manipulate the mind of his audience was what mattered most. He didn't care about the size of the audience. Leaving one person in wonder was just as satisfying as captivating a whole auditorium filled with spectators.

These feelings were not new. They had been growing for the last few months and now seemed to be climaxing in his heart. He didn't want to perform tonight. It would be another bored audience that was saturated with all the hype of the casinos. Many of them had probably already seen his show and most of his tricks. His manager always told him that he exaggerated everything in his mind and that the show was going great. Charles wished he could believe this.

The scotch steadied his nerves. He poured another glass and drank it slowly, savoring the taste. Alcohol seemed to be his only comfort these last few months. Magic had lost its edge here in Reno, under the big lights. He longed for a different setting, but knew that his manager, who was just as bored as he was, would be calling him at any moment. He would have to go through another round of mundane rehearsals very shortly.

Charles wondered how he was going to make it through many more months of this. He opened a big bottom drawer in his desk and fished for an old flask he had kept from his college days. He didn't see it anywhere and wondered why he had kept so much junk in the first place. In anger he pulled the drawer completely out and started shaking it upside down on the floor. The full contents of the drawer scattered along the floor. Emptying it out, he threw the drawer against his wall and sat back down, frustrated out of his mind.

This week was getting to him. He breathed deeply, trying to calm himself. What was he going to do? He couldn't go on like this, performing every night for these mindless audiences. He felt like a caged bird that couldn't escape, running from side-to-side looking through the bars, wondering how to get out. He was trapped.

It was in this moment of silence and frustration that Chesterton looked in the pile of junk on his floor and saw something. He turned his head to the side to get a better look at it. He extended his hand through the pile and reached for it, gently picking it up and holding it up to the light.

It was a ring. One he hadn't seen in a long time. He had forgotten all about it. It brought back many memories. It reminded him of a quieter life, one where magic left him in wonder; a life where people were amazed by his tricks. A life where he would no longer feel like a caged bird; trapped! This could be the answer he was looking for, his ticket to freedom. He wanted it and was ready to do whatever it took to get back to the wonder of magic. This was his chance.

He quickly picked up his desk phone and dialed for his manager. It was two rings before he heard an answer. "Rodriguez, we need to talk," Chesterton said, urgently.

Chapter 1

—◦◦◦◦◦◦◦◦◦—

Aɴᴅʀᴇᴡ Sᴛᴇᴠᴇɴsᴏɴ ᴀᴘᴘʀᴏᴀᴄʜᴇᴅ ʜɪs ᴄᴀʀ. He hoped his new friend would like it. It wasn't anything fancy, just a Ford Mustang, a couple years old. He kept it nice and clean, and he was sure to give it a good wax job every couple months. To him it looked just right; silver with a black racing stripe down the side. It took him two summers of work to save up the money to buy it. His parents had it detailed for him as a graduation present. He opened the driver's side door and slid in. Looking in the rearview mirror he adjusted his glasses, and then checked his light brown hair, making sure the part was perfect. Appearance was everything. He wanted these guys to approve of him. He didn't want anything going wrong with his first impression.

It was bad enough living at home his freshman year. Andrew wanted the experience of a typical college kid. He wanted the parties, the fun, and possibly a little drinking mixed in there too. He hated that his first year of college was just about over and he hadn't made many friends. Sure, he made good grades and was able to save a lot of money living at home, but he wanted more. Being nineteen and in his first year of college was supposed to be one of the best years of his life. So far, it was one Andrew was ready to forget.

Early in the semester things started to change when Andrew met Johnny Platt. He was known as the most popular student at Eastern Iowa University where they both attended. Located on the outskirts of Waterloo, Iowa, Eastern Iowa was known for its farming sciences. Most of the students who picked the school usually hoped to move back home and to continue working on their family farms.

Johnny Platt was not a typical student. Everyone on campus knew who he was. He was known for his wild parties and for pulling clever pranks on the faculty. All the professors knew he was behind them, but there was never any hard evidence to pin his name to any of the antics. His pranks ran the gamut from tame to outrageous. He occasionally broke into professors' cars and covered the interior with shaving cream, mud, or even frogs. His most recent prank included hacking into the school's main computer system and clearing most of his student debt off the books. Through his methods, he was able to get exams postponed and school days canceled. Anyone who was a friend of Johnny's had instant access to popularity and power on campus.

Andrew and Johnny were in the same Physics class this current semester. The professor had randomly assigned them to be lab partners. They started out purely as acquaintances, but quickly developed a friendship. Andrew, seizing the opportunity of befriending Johnny, did most of his work, even volunteering to do Johnny's homework for other classes. Andrew knew this was his big opportunity to harness some fame on campus.

Tonight Andrew was heading over to Johnny's dorm room. This was the first time he'd been invited to hang out outside of class. There was no organized party tonight on campus, but one could be assured that any social gathering Johnny attended could easily spring into a wild party at any moment. Andrew could only hope.

Pulling into campus, Andrew found an empty spot near Johnny's dorm room. He checked his hair one last time before exiting the car. As he reached for his door handle he could see that his hand was shaking with nerves. He couldn't believe he was actually going to hang out with Johnny Platt. Getting out of his car, he shut the door and pressed his electronic key to lock it.

Johnny lived on the third floor. The dorm building was commonly known as "Johnny's building" among the students. Andrew walked up the two flights of steps, trying to control his nerves. He wanted to be cool, calm, and ready for anything that might happen tonight. The hall was exceptionally clean for a college dormitory. He quickly found Johnny's door. Holding his breath, he lifted his arm and knocked a couple times on the door.

"Hey, who's there!" a voice said from the inside. It wasn't Johnny. Whoever it was had a strong New York accent, and at the moment seemed quite abrasive.

"Umm, hey, this is Andrew... Andrew Stevenson. Johnny invited me. Is he here?" Andrew said tensely.

He could tell people in the room were talking about who he was and trying to decide if they should let him in or not. After a few seconds Andrew could hear the inside locks on the door unlocking.

When the door opened, Andrew could see that the New York accent came from a short Italian looking fellow, who could be no taller than 5'3. He was stocky. He had dark hair, including a mustache. He looked like he was acting as the bodyguard to Johnny's dorm room. Andrew had seen him around campus.

"Come on in...I'm Frankie," said the short greeter.

"Thanks," Andrew said, walking into the room. It was filled with smoke. He stepped further into the living area.

"Hey, come on in, man!" the all too familiar voice said. Johnny was lounged on his couch with a beer in his hand and a cigarette in the other. He quickly brushed aside his blond shaggy hair to get a good fix on Andrew. "How's my favorite lab partner?"

"I'm doing great, Johnny, thanks for having me. I appreciate it." Andrew's eyes were fixed on the girl sitting closely beside Johnny. Her name was Angela and just like Johnny she was known by many on campus, but not for her pranks. She was known for her pure beauty. She was a very tall, tan, college senior. She sat in the front in Andrew's American history class. Guys were always coming up to her before and after class, trying to land a date with her. Andrew never bothered to try to talk to her as he knew she was way out of his league. He never imagined that he would actually get a chance to talk to her. At the present moment Johnny had his arm resting comfortably around her. She was dressed casually in jeans and an Eastern Iowa t-shirt.

"Andrew, have you met Angela?" Johnny asked.

"Umm, no I haven't actually. Hi, I'm Andrew," he answered, extending his hand.

Angela chuckled a little at the formality of it all. "Well, pleased to meet you, Andrew," she said reaching for his hand. Her hand felt soft.

Johnny spoke up, "Try to relax, Andrew. We're just here hanging out, having a good time. No need to be worried. Frankie and I just plan on kickin' back tonight, hittin' a few beers, maybe catchin' a flick later, nothing major, just takin' it easy, you know what I'm sayin'."

"Yeah, no problem, man, I just wanted to check out your place and see what was up." Andrew said, trying to sound casual.

"All right, cool…you want a beer?" Johnny asked.

"Uhh, maybe…sure, why not," Andrew said, stuttering over his words. Andrew had only tried alcohol once a few years ago, and it did not turn out well for him. His parents caught him sharing a bottle of wine in a back room at church. He was severely grounded.

"Frankie, go grab Andrew a beer, man."

"We're out of beer. Remember you sold a case to those high school kids yesterday," Frankie answered, sounding a little upset.

"All right, well, go check with Dax next door." Frankie got up and left the room on his hunt for more beer.

"So Andrew, what do you do? What are you studying?" Angela spoke, nuzzling up closer to Johnny. Even her voice was so pleasantly attractive. Andrew found it mesmerizing.

"Well, I'm a, actually, um…I'm actually studying Mechanical Engineering,"

Angela's eyes got wide. "Oh, wow, it looks like Johnny finally found a friend who really studies," she said, patting her man gently on the chest.

"Don't be dissin' my man Andrew," Johnny spoke up with a smile, "he's got me out of a couple binds already. He's been a lifesaver in Lab." Johnny leaned forward to give Andrew a fist pound. It felt good being so readily accepted. With basically no friends at the university, Andrew was beginning to feel like he hit the jackpot with his new friendship.

Angela continued, "So, Andrew, is there any lucky lady in your life?"

Andrew looked at the ground, shaking his head and smiling, "No, not really, but you know, I'm always keeping my eyes open."

Johnny laughed a little, "That a boy! We'll help you catch one eventually, man."

After a few minutes Frankie arrived back, apparently with Dax. Walking in the room, Andrew had to take a second glance. Dax was tall. Andrew guessed he had to be at least 6'5. He was skinny with a shaved head. It was quite a sight seeing him with Frankie, who was more than a full foot shorter in height.

Dax was the first to speak, and it was clear he was upset, "Johnny, you drank all my beer, man! Remember? How am I ever supposed to keep it stocked at the rate you drink it? You're going to have to move up to Milwaukee someday with all the beer you drink." Andrew could tell right away that Dax was an Iowa farm boy. He thought he could recognize one anywhere.

"All right, quit your clowning, Dax, I'll make it up to you somehow," Johnny said, "Just let me figure out something."

"Dude, you never repay me, and you're always stealing my beer and taking stuff from my room. You owe me big, man, for all the stuff you've took." It surprised Andrew to hear another student talking to Johnny so boldly.

Johnny removed his arm from around Angela. He leaned forward slightly in his seat. "Well, name your price. I want to show you, Dax, that I mean it this time. What do you want?"

"I don't know man…something big though…"

Johnny breathed deeply under his breath. He ran his fingers through his shaggy hair, trying to think of something on the spot. He continued on, "How about this, I'll take you out tomorrow and we'll hit the casino. We'll throw back a couple drinks at the bar, play some cards, and maybe catch a show. What do you think?"

"All right, that's a good start, man," Dax said nodding his head in agreement, "but it'll have to be tomorrow. I'm going to hit the court tonight with some of the guys."

"Okay, so are we cool?" Johnny said, extending his hand out to Dax.

"Yeah, man," Dax answered, shaking hands with Johnny, "but why do you want to go a show? What's up with that?"

"Angela here wants to go see this new magician guy they got out there." Johnny reached toward a nearby coffee table and grabbed a glossy flyer. He held it up for everyone to see. "*The Amazing Charles Chesterton's Show of Magic and Wonder,*" Johnny read from the flyer.

"I've heard it's a great show. I had a couple girlfriends go see him last week and they said it's definitely worth seeing," Angela said with excitement.

"Johnny, are you sure this is something you want to waste your time on? This sounds like kid tricks or something. I mean, Charles Chesterton? Even his name sounds lame," Dax said skeptically.

"Cm' on, man, it'll be fine. I scored a bunch of tickets with some inside connections. I'll take a few and then we'll scalp the rest. How bad can it be?" Johnny said. He then fixed his gaze on Andrew, "Listen, Drew, you think you can find a girl before tomorrow?"

Andrew was shocked. His eyes got a little wider. He wasn't used to being called Drew, and he was surprised and excited to be invited. "Yeah, um, maybe…I'll see what I can do, you know, sometimes it's not easy finding someone on such short notice and…"

"Who is this kid?" Dax interrupted. He had a confused look on his face.

"Oh, sorry, Dax. This is Andrew, or Drew, whatever. My lab partner," Johnny answered.

"Pleased to meet you," Andrew said, extending his hand to shake.

Dax looked to be both confused and disgusted at the same time. It was like he thought Johnny was too good to be entertaining nerds like Andrew. He just shook his head, leaving Andrew's hand out in front of him. Andrew felt very embarrassed. He quickly retreated from the shake. Even though Frankie and Angela quickly accepted Andrew, it appeared as though it would take some time to win over Dax.

Johnny spoke up, "All right, guys, we'll plan to meet here tomorrow at about six-thirty and go from there. Dax, I'll have all the money we need for a good time. You just show up, man, and be ready to party, and Drew, you work on finding that girl, man. It's going to be a good night."

Andrew drove home excited out of his mind. He didn't stay at the dorm very long. They mostly sat around and listened to Johnny tell the story of when he covered the Dean's floor with Crisco. He almost got caught until he paid off an underclassman to take the blame for him. It was a great story, and it was quite interesting to hear about how Johnny was able to obtain the key to the Dean's office and later maneuver his way past security into the office. It sounded like a story from a Navy Seal expedition. Andrew and Frankie held onto every word as it was told.

Andrew couldn't help but feel that he was accepted. He was now in with Johnny Platt. There was no telling how far this friendship would go. Never in his life had Andrew been a popular kid, and he was always looking for ways to impress people. He bought the best clothes and made sure his car was always in top shape, but in the end he felt like it had gotten him nowhere. Most weekends were spent at home with his family, or possibly attending some lame church event with his folks. Andrew knew this was the beginning of a new life for himself.

The one thing Andrew was worried about was the necessity of finding a girl, based on Johnny's comment. Andrew wasn't sure where to look. He didn't know any girls on campus, and there weren't any from his high school days that he was interested in. He wondered if Johnny would be upset if he showed up alone. Sure, it was just an offhand comment Johnny made, but Andrew didn't want to disappoint Johnny whatsoever.

Thinking through the list of possible girls, Andrew's mind kept going back to a girl at his church. Her name was Sophia. She was a home-schooled high school senior. Her parents were best friends with Andrew's. He had always found her somewhat attractive, but thought she was a little too plain for his taste. His parents would occasionally encourage him to ask her out. Andrew never seriously considered it until now. He needed a girl and he needed one fast. Even though he wasn't crazy about Sophia, he thought she would do for now.

He pulled into his home just past 10:00 p.m. He parked right beside his dad's truck. He turned the engine off and sat back in his seat, resting from all the excitement. Looking in the rearview mirror, he couldn't help but smile at himself as he fixed his hair.

Chapter 2

———∿∿⌒⊙⌒⊙⌒⊙⌒∿∿———

ANDREW SLEPT IN JUST A little. The April sun was peeking through the bedroom curtains. He felt well rested. He thought he ought to get started on the day. There were a couple of English papers that he had been putting off for a while that he needed to get started on. He also wanted to be sure he had plenty of time to get ready for tonight. It was going to be a good night.

He reached over to his dresser and grabbed his glasses. The world became clear. He quickly slid his feet out of bed onto the floor. Standing up, he stretched his arms out wide.

On the way to the bathroom, he passed his mom going into the kitchen. "Good morning, sunshine," she said sarcastically.

"Hey," he answered. The morning was the only time of day when Andrew's appearance was not 'perfect.' His hair was a mess, and he always wore an old pair of mesh shorts around the house, along with a Chicago Bulls t-shirt. He would never dare to leave the house or let anyone see him in his sleeping attire. He constantly thought about his appearance and the image he portrayed. He took a long shower and got himself ready for the day. His hair needed a little extra time this morning.

As he entered the kitchen, he noticed the house was quiet. He figured his dad had his usual errands he had to run, and was probably working at the church or visiting a widow in need. A few months back Andrew's dad, Jerry, was appointed as a new deacon at the church. He took the job very seriously and was usually gone early on Saturday mornings to help someone in need. Andrew never said anything, but he secretly admired his dad for his servant's attitude. He was always thinking of others before himself. It was a wonderful virtue.

Andrew sat down at the dining room table and poured himself a bowl of Lucky Charms. He dove his spoon deep into the cereal and started to eat when he noticed something in the driveway, or rather didn't notice something. His car was gone! Where could it be? His dad's truck was gone as well, so he knew his dad hadn't taken it. He worried about his car constantly and hoped it hadn't been stolen in the night.

He could see his mom, Diane, walk into the living room. At the moment she was putting on a pair of fancy earrings. Much like Andrew, she was always well kept, and wanted to look her best before she left the house. He called out to her, "Mom... hey Mom, where's my car?"

"Oh, it's ok, Son, Elliot took it this morning. He said he had to meet a friend to work on a science project together," she said nonchalantly. Andrew couldn't believe what he had just heard. His younger brother, Elliot, was not supposed to touch his car. Andrew had let him borrow it once to drive himself to school for basketball practice; he didn't want the hassle of having to drive back and forth to pick him up, so he just figured he'd let Elliot take the car that one time. Andrew now realized that had been a mistake.

He answered in anger, "What in the world! Why did he do that? I didn't tell him he could use my car! What was he thinking?"

"Calm down, Andrew," his mother said, finishing with her earrings, "I'm sure he will be back before too long. Just don't worry about it."

"Listen, Mom, he knows he is not supposed to take my car. It is my car!" Elliot was sixteen now, and Andrew thought his younger brother was always interfering in his life. He looked up to Andrew, and he was always looking for ways to hang out with his older brother. Elliot most likely took the car to show off to his friends. Andrew was extremely angry.

"Andrew, I'm sorry he took your car without asking. Dad and I will talk to him about it when he comes home. Elliot's a pretty good driver and he was not going far. I'm sure everything is going to be just fine."

"All right, well, he's going to have to learn not to fool around with my stuff anymore," he said, emphatically.

"I'm sure we will work it all out later. Listen, I'm going to head over to Grandma's house and we're going to hit a few stores at the mall. I should be back by the middle of the afternoon. There are some leftovers in the fridge you can heat up. Dad shouldn't be gone too long either."

"Ok, sounds good," Andrew said, feeling somewhat relieved that his mom and dad would reprimand Elliot when he came home.

"Take care. I'll see you this afternoon."

"Oh, one more thing Mom. I'm going to be out with friends tonight, so don't wait on me for dinner," Andrew said, feeling proud of his plans.

"Friends? Which friends?" said Diane, surprised.

"Just some guys I met at school. They're in my physics class."

"Ok, cool! What do you think you will be up to?"

"Oh, nothing much, just catching a bite to eat and hanging out," Andrew answered, lying to his mother. He knew she would never approve of him attending a show at the casino.

"That sounds fantastic! You have fun and be safe. I'll see you later," she responded, excited by the idea of Andrew having friends.

"Bye, Mom!"

Andrew wasn't able to get much work done on his English papers. It was approaching noon and he wondered when he should call Sophia. He figured it was a sure lock that she would go out with him if he told her it was just as friends. Over the past few years they had hung out together on various youth group trips and church events, so going to the magic show tonight would be only a little suspicious.

He picked up his phone and searched through his contacts. It was getting late into the morning and he figured he better give her a call before she made her own plans. Andrew wiped his forehead, realizing that he was sweating just a little. It wasn't so much the idea of asking Sophia out, but rather the whole structure of his plans. He wanted to impress his new friends and he was hoping that everything with Sophia would fall right in line.

He found her name and pushed the call button. He waited. It rang once…twice… They had talked a couple times on the phone over the years, so he hoped Sophia wouldn't be caught too off guard by his call.

"Hello," he heard from the other end. Her voice always sounded confident, but definitely feminine.

"Oh, hey Sophia, this is Andrew, Andrew Stevenson. You know from church."

"Yeah, I know who you are, Andrew. How's it going?" Sophia responded, quickly noticing his nervousness.

"I'm doing well. I'm just hanging out at the house, trying to get some school work done. How are you?"

"I'm fine, thank you. I'm here at the park spending some time with a couple of my younger brothers. What's up?" Andrew was always impressed by her poise.

"Well, If it's all right with you, I wondering if you might possibly be interested in maybe doing something tonight," he said.

"Yeah, I'm up for doing something, but you need to be a little more clear, Andrew."

"Well… yeah… see… and you know that's why I was thinking maybe me and you could go see a movie or something."

"Ok… Is this like a date or something, Andrew?" Sophia responded, being very direct with her questions.

"No, no… no, no date! We're just hanging out as friends like old times."

"Andrew, we've never hung out outside of youth group. I'll go see a movie with you, but I'm not sure what this is about."

"It's just hanging out. I don't have anything to do tonight and I was wondering if you wanted to catch that new Superheroes flick?" Andrew said, trying to reassure her. He wasn't sure how he would cover up this lie later, but at the moment it didn't matter to him.

"Ok, Andrew, I'll see it with you, but you have to promise me that this isn't a date."

"It isn't a date. I'm just looking for a friend to see the movie with," Andrew said, getting a little upset.

"All right, what time should I be ready?"

"6:30."

"Cool, well, I better get going. My little brother wants me to help him up the slide, but I'll see you tonight."

"Sounds good. Take care, Sophia."

"Bye," she said, hanging up the phone. Andrew jumped up in excitement. He pumped his fist. He was excited everything with Sophia had fallen into place. He thought about how impressed the guys would be that he found a girl on such short notice. His lie about the movie would have to be something he would work out later, but for right now he didn't care. He was just excited Sophia had agreed to his plan.

It was approaching 2:00 p.m. and Andrew wondered where his brother could be. He was getting anxious. The car would need to be cleaned again before picking up Sophia. He thought if everything went well tonight, then Johnny and his friends would be sure to accept him as a regular around the dorm. There were many preparations he needed to make before the evening.

As the minutes passed Andrew grew more and more angry. How could his brother do such a thing? Elliot knew he was not supposed to take the car. Where could he be? From what his mom said, it sounded like he should've been back hours ago. Andrew tried to distract himself with various chores around the house, but it was all in vain. He ended up sitting at the kitchen table staring out the window, hoping his brother would pull in at any moment.

While he was daydreaming, a car pulled into his driveway, but it was his dad's old pickup. Andrew thought he would recognize that 1990 white Toyota anywhere. His dad climbed out of the driver's seat and walked up their front steps. He was dirty; he looked as if he had been crawling around in the mud. Upon entering the house, he took off his shoes in order to not track in any mud.

Andrew's dad, Jerry, was a large man. He measured about six feet, four inches in height, and probably weighed about 275 pounds; most of the weight was pure muscle mass. He kept himself in great shape, but not because of any gym membership, but because he was a hard worker. He owned his own carpentry business and worked around fifty hours a week. Seemingly never to grow tired, he even spent a lot of his time and energy working at their church. He volunteered in almost every capacity: maintenance, service, helping widows, and even occasionally speaking when the pastor was sick or out of town. Jerry Stevenson was known for having a servant's heart.

He saw Andrew sitting idly by the kitchen table as he walked in the house. "Hello Son, how ya doin'?" he said, speaking through his thick beard.

"I'm doing all right. I'm waiting for Elliot to get home. He took my car this morning without asking and I'm hoping he'll get back soon," Andrew said with condemnation in his voice.

"Oh, I imagine he won't be too long. Elliot's pretty good about returning what he borrows," said Jerry, not seeming the least bit concerned.

"Yeah… what've you been up to, Dad? You look filthy."

His dad chuckled just a little. "I was helping Mrs. Walters with her plumbing this morning. Her pipes are so old they were practically falling apart. I was trying to unclog a blockage when a joint broke free and sewage spilled all over me. It was a terrible mess."

At that moment, Andrew realized that it was not dirt that his dad was covered in. He thought he was going to be sick. Jerry continued, "But bless her heart, Mrs. Walters is such a sweet lady. I feel bad for her. Her kids never seem to visit her. She just gets so lonely."

"Well, I'm glad you are here for her, Dad. I'm sure she appreciates all you do for her."

"Yeah, thanks, Son! Well, I'd better shower. I'm excited for the big game tonight. I can't remember the last time I was this excited for a hockey game. This is going to be great."

Andrew froze, slapping his hand over his forehead. He couldn't believe he had forgotten. His dad had been looking forward to this night for a long time. He had scored some playoff tickets for the local Waterloo hockey team and had been planning for the two of them to go to out for a guys' dinner of wings before attending the hockey game. His dad was so excited to spend an evening with his son.

Andrew felt horrible. He truly respected and admired his father, and he felt as if he was always disappointing him. His father was always very patient with Andrew and most of the time gave him lots of grace. He was a very forgiving man. Andrew was so upset with himself for forgetting about these plans.

Instantly Jerry could tell something was not right, "What's wrong, Son?"

"Oh Dad, I'm so sorry. I made plans for tonight," Andrew thought he would just face the situation head on. "Yeah, I told some guys I'd get together with them and just hang out. I'm sorry Dad, we might have to reschedule."

Jerry was still calm, "Son, we can't reschedule. Playoff tickets are hard to get. You know we've been planning this for a long time. I just mainly wanted to spend some time with you. I've haven't seen much of you lately."

"I know, Dad. I wish things hadn't worked out like this, but there is nothing I can do. I'm sorry, I'll try to make it up to you sometime."

His dad looked defeated, like the wind had just been knocked out of him, "Well, ok, I, umm, guess Elliot and I can go again."

"Thanks, Dad, like I said, next week sometime let's go out and try to hit the driving range or something like that. It'll be fun."

"Ok, sounds good," his dad said, sounding utterly disappointed. He continued, "Look, I'm going to go ahead and jump in the shower. If you see Elliot, just let him know that your ticket is now available. He'll probably want to go."

"All right, Dad, I'll let him know," Andrew returned. He felt so horrible for letting down his father in this way. His dad was a gentle giant who worked hard at not raising his voice and staying calm. Early in his life he had been known for having a temper and getting into trouble. Andrew didn't know much of his father's past, but from the bits and pieces he'd picked up over the years, he knew that his father was a man people didn't want to mess with. His father would only say that his life and who he was had dramatically changed in his mid-twenties. He became heavily involved in his church and it was at that time that he met Diane, Andrew's mother.

Andrew was always curious about his father's past. Over the past few years he had tried to discreetly pry any info he could from his grandparents about his father. He never gained much ground with them. In some of his most desperate times of curiosity he would search through the attic or some of his dad's personal things to see if there was anything to give him a clue. Overall, all of Andrew's attempts turned up empty.

He was lost in a daydream when he saw his brother pull into the driveway with his car. All of Andrew's anger instantly returned. Elliot was going to get a piece of his mind. He quickly got up from the table and raced toward the front door. Quickly opening the door, he threw himself outside. Elliot was just exiting the car. He was all decked out in his skater clothes and looked as if he'd been at the skate park all morning.

Andrew was the first to speak, "Elliot, what do you think you're doing? You know you're not supposed to take my car. What's the matter with you?"

"Listen Andrew, I'm sorry, I didn't think you'd mind and..." he said bashfully.

"What do you mean I wouldn't mind? Of course I mind. This is my car, you idiot! What if something had happened?"

Elliot stood there in silence. He dropped his head as if he was ashamed of his actions. Andrew thought this was odd, and wondered what was wrong with his brother. He thought maybe Elliot was hiding something from him.

Andrew went to inspect his car and then he realized what had happened.

Chapter 3

—⁓⌇⌖⌇⁓—

"WHAT HAVE YOU DONE?" ANDREW yelled, stepping closer to his brother.

Elliot put his hands up in a defensive position, "Listen, I'm so sorry. I don't know what I was thinking."

"You don't know what you were thinking? Is that all you have to say about this?" Andrew said, pointing at the large dent and busted headlight on the right side of his car. There was also a large amount of blue painted rubbed onto the front of it.

"I was out with the guys and I had to make a sharp turn. I thought I could make it but I ended up hitting the corner of a stupid dumpster."

Andrew looked closely at the damage. His heart sank. Not only was the car ruined for the evening, but it would also have to be in the shop for about a week. He was looking forward to picking Sophia up in it and showing it off to the guys. His whole plan was wrecked. He didn't know what to do. He became angrier by the moment.

Elliot didn't know what to say. He tried to calm his brother down, "Andrew, I'm sorry, man, I just wasn't thinking. I probably should've been more careful."

"Wasn't thinking?" Andrew couldn't contain himself. In a rage of anger, he stepped toward Elliot and with one quick motion he reared his fist back and punched his brother square in the nose.

"Aww!" Elliot yelled, falling to the ground, grabbing his nose. Moaning in pain, he began rolling back and forth on the ground. Tears welled up in his eyes from the pain. Andrew could see blood starting to pool in the palm of his brother's hand.

He walked back to car, assessing the damage. *He is going to pay for this*, Andrew thought. He felt like Elliot was always getting in the way, and this time he had gone too far. Andrew felt justified in punching his brother. He had it coming, and needed to be taught a lesson. Hopefully this time Elliot would remember not to touch his car.

As all this was happening their mother, Diane, pulled into the driveway and parked beside Andrew's Mustang. She quickly got out and ran over to Elliot, lying in the front lawn.

"Elliot, Elliot, what's going on?" She bent over her son and noticed the blood pouring from his hand onto the grass. She tried to pull his hand away in order to assess the damage done. Elliot gave no response. He just kept moaning in pain, holding tight to his nose.

She looked at Andrew, trying to get an answer from him, "What happened? Why's his nose bleeding? Andrew, what's going on?"

"You need to ask him," Andrew shot back. "He just pulled into the driveway with my car looking like this," Andrew said, pointing to his car.

Diane looked up from her son to see the damage done to the front of Andrew's car. A puzzled look formed on her face, wondering what had happened. She continued, "Andrew, are you saying he hurt himself in an accident?"

"Well, not exactly," Andrew answered, not knowing what to say.

"Listen, Andrew, please tell me what happened. Why is your brother bleeding this badly? Should we call an ambulance?"

At that moment Elliot began to stand slowly. His mother grabbed his arm, trying to lift him onto his feet. The blood flow was slowing. Diane reached into her purse, pulling out a few tissues. She cupped them over Elliot's nose to absorb some of the blood. He quickly pushed her hand away, squeezing the tissues against his face.

Diane continued, frantically looking for answers, "Honey, are you ok? Do we need to go the hospital? Please tell me what happened."

"Listen, Mom," Elliot spoke, pulling the tissues from his face, "I just borrowed Andrew's car. I don't know what I was thinking. I mean, I was going to show it to my friends, I didn't think Andrew would mind and…"

Andrew interrupted. "You didn't think I would mind?" He said, shouting. "This is my car! You know how much work and money I have put into this thing! You know better than to do something like this."

"Andrew, calm down for just a second," his mother said, trying to ease the tension in the air. "He's trying to explain what happened."

"No, it's ok, Mom. I took his car," Elliot explained, "I wasn't supposed to. I was just trying to impress my friends. I really shouldn't have."

"Well, please tell me how this happened!" His mother demanded.

Elliot continued, "I was trying to make a sharp turn and I thought I could make it, but there was this big blue dumpster sitting in my way. I didn't turn sharp enough and smashed right into the corner of it. I'm sorry."

"Is that when you hit your nose?" his mom asked. This question caught Elliot off guard. He thought for a second or two before answering.

"Yeah... yeah, that's what happened. I, umm, when I hit the dumpster, it was kind of sudden and my face went forward and it hit the steering wheel. My nose just started bleeding."

Andrew couldn't believe what he had just heard. He was stunned. Elliot took the fall for him. He knew his brother admired him, but this was incredible. Andrew couldn't imagine what would have happened if Elliot had told the truth. His parents would've probably made him cover the cost of the medical bills. He was completely shocked by his brother.

Their father walked casually out of the house, towel in hand. He was barefoot and wearing a pair of green sweatpants and an undershirt. He had heard all the commotion outside and thought he would check on what was transpiring.

"Hey, is everything ok? Elliot, what happened to your face?" He could see the stains of blood under his nose and on his shirt.

Diane answered, "Elliot had an accident in the Mustang. He wasn't being careful and crashed into a dumpster."

"How about the nose? What happened with that?"

"He hit it against the steering wheel during the crash," Diane answered.

Their father seemed puzzled. Right away, he knew something didn't add up. "Where is this dumpster that you hit, son?"

Elliot looked up at his father, "It's over by the skate park on Fletcher Street. It's sitting right there by the entrance."

Jerry knew his kids well enough to know when they were lying. Also, there were holes in the story. The skate park was at least a ten minute drive from their house, and there would have been a lot of blood in the car and on his clothing if he had bled from the park to their house. Jerry looked over at the dent in the car, studying the damage, and then looked up at Andrew, making direct eye contact. Andrew knew his father didn't believe Elliot's story.

Jerry Stevenson stood in silence for a few moments before speaking. He was calm. "Well, Elliot, why don't you head into the house and get yourself cleaned up, then I'll look at your nose and see if it's broken. I'll deal with the car tomorrow afternoon."

The two parents were the first to step into the house. As Andrew was walking up the front steps, Elliot turned to face his brother. He thought it would be a good opportunity to offer Andrew another apology, "Look, man, once again, I can't believe I did this. I will make it up to you."

Andrew stood looking at his brother. He didn't know how to respond. He appreciated his brother taking the fall for him, but he was not in the mood for an apology. He was not going to forgive his brother this easily.

Elliot continued, "Andrew, I can't believe I crashed your car. I should have never taken it. I'm sorry, man! I'm so sorry for what I've done."

Andrew looked straight at his brother, emotionless. "You'd better be sorry!" he answered, walking into the house.

Andrew hit the steering wheel in his dad's truck as he drove. He was angry and frustrated. This night was supposed to be perfect. He couldn't believe he was driving an old dented pick-up truck to the casino tonight. He wanted so badly to be completely accepted by the guys. Even though Johnny seemed to be accepting of him, he didn't want to mess anything up. Being a friend of Johnny's meant instant popularity on campus, and that was something Andrew coveted.

Approaching a red light, he stopped. Just a couple more blocks to Sophia's house. Looking into the rearview mirror, he checked his hair. He hoped Sophia would be pleased with his appearance. He liked her, and he always appreciated her confidence. The light turned to green and he was on his way.

Pulling up to her house, he saw her mother outside, watching a couple of her younger siblings. He paralleled parked on the side of the street. Checking his hair one more time, Andrew opened the door and got out of the truck. It was a beautiful Iowa evening. The temperature was in the mid seventies and the sun was still shining brightly. Andrew could hear birds chirping as he approached the house.

"Hello, Andrew," said Sophia's mom. She was lounging in a lawn chair, perfectly relaxed.

"Hey Mrs. Mitchell, how are you today?" Andrew returned, not making eye contact.

"I'm doing fine, thank you. I'm just enjoying this beautiful day and making sure little Bobby and Ethan don't kill each other," she said, pointing to the two little ones playing roughly in the yard.

Andrew chuckled a little under his breath, "Well, is Sophia around?"

"Sure, she's inside. She's probably just finishing up the dishes. You may want to knock on the door and just make sure she knows you're here."

"Ok, thanks," Andrew returned. He walked up the front steps to the house and knocked on the door. He noticed his hands were a little sweaty. He quickly wiped them against his pants.

"I'll get it," he heard a voice call from inside. Andrew heard footsteps approaching.

The door opened and Andrew came face-to-face with Sophia's dad. He was a cheerful man and had a big smile on his face through a thick mustache. "Well, it's nice to see you Andy, how ya' doing this fine evening?"

"I'm doing fine, sir, thank you." Even though Mr. Mitchell was a cheerful man, it was still intimidating speaking with Sophia's father.

"Well, Sophia tells me you guys are going to see that new superhero movie. Which theater do you think you'll go to?" asked Mr. Mitchell. This question hit Andrew like a ton of bricks. He had completely forgotten about the lie he told. He didn't know how he was going to work this out. The incident with Elliot completely took his mind off of his lie. He actually hadn't thought about it since he got off the phone with Sophia. He stood stunned for a couple of seconds in silence. He started to sweat.

"You ok, son?" Mr. Mitchell asked, seeing Andrew panic.

"Umm, yeah, I'm fine. I'm just…um…a little warm that's all. I…um…think we'll go to the mall theater. That one's pretty nice, I think." Andrew said, stuttering over his words.

Mr. Mitchell put his hand on Andrew's shoulder and looked directly into his eyes, "Listen son, there's nothing to be worried about. Sophia says this is just a couple friends gettin' together. Don't get yourself all worked up over this. You're a good kid. You just need to remember as long as you keep your hands and your lips to yourself, everything should work out just fine."

"Umm, yes sir," Andrew said looking at the ground. He didn't care how direct Mr. Mitchell's words were, he was still trying to figure out how to work out this lie with Sophia.

"Hey, what's up, Andrew!" Sophia said, coming out of the house. She was dressed casually. Her blonde hair was flowing freely.

"H... H... Hey!" Andrew answered, clearly with nerves in his voice. Sophia could also see the sweat on his forehead.

"What's gotten into you? We're just going out as friends, right?" she said with a puzzled look on her face. Her dad smiled in approval.

"Yeah, I don't know. I guess it's just a little hot out here or something like that. But I'm fine, really," Andrew said, wiping his forehead.

"Ok, well if you say so," Sophia said, shrugging her shoulders. "I'll see you later, Dad, I don't think we should be gone too long."

"Sounds good! You kids have fun, you hear?"

"We will!" Sophia said, walking down the steps.

On his way back to the truck, Andrew wondered how he'd ever break the news to Sophia that they were actually going to the casino. Her dad would never approve of this. He wondered what would happen if Mr. Mitchell were ever to find out about Andrew's intentions.

Andrew climbed into the truck. He didn't bother to open the door for Sophia, as she seemed very opposed to the idea of a date in any form or fashion. Climbing into the cab, Sophia spoke up, "Andrew, what happened to the Mustang? I was looking forward to riding in your fancy car. What's up?"

"Yeah, it's got a couple problems. I thought it'd be best to leave it home tonight," Andrew answered, fishing for words. He didn't want to get into the whole ordeal of Elliot crashing it. He had enough to worry about.

"Oh, well, sorry to hear that."

"Thanks," Andrew said in approval. He drove away from Sophia's house. The car was silent for a few minutes. Sophia occupied herself by looking out the passenger side window, waving at neighbors. The town of Waterloo had endured a harsh winter, filled with lots of snow. Residents were always very anxious to get outside once the weather became nice.

After a few miles Sophia noticed that Andrew was not driving in the direction of the theater. She broke the silence, "Andrew, I don't know what way you're taking. It would have been a whole lot faster to just drive through town, instead of heading toward the highway. It's like you're going to the opposite end of town."

Andrew pulled into the parking lot of a nearby restaurant. He shut the engine off and breathed deeply, wondering how he was going to explain this to Sophia. She spoke up, "Andrew, what are you doing? Why'd you park here?"

"Listen," Andrew hesitated, "I think I better tell you this now. I, or we, are not going to the movies."

"What are you talking about? That's what you told me!"

"I know. Look, I told some guys I would hang out with them tonight, and they told me to bring a friend. I thought it was something you might want to do so I thought I would invite you to hang out with us."

"So you lied to me!" Sophia said angrily, looking straight at Andrew.

"I know, and I'm sorry. I just really needed someone to bring along tonight. I thought you'd be the perfect person and..."

"I can't believe you," Sophia said, shaking her head.

"Sophia, I'm sorry I lied to you, but I really didn't want to let these guys down. These are some of the most popular guys at Eastern Iowa."

"Andrew, you know you have a problem? Don't you?"

"Yeah, I know, I lied to you."

"No, I mean bigger than that," she said, looking directly at Andrew. "You are always trying to impress people. It's like you will go to any cost just to gain a little popularity or something like that. You don't want people to see that your life is imperfect, that you don't always have it all together."

Andrew knew she was probably right, but thought that there was nothing he could do about it at the moment. He continued, "Listen Sophia, all I can say at this point is that I'm sorry. I'll make this up to you. Please, just go along with me in this, and in the end it won't be a big deal. It's just us hanging out with a couple other guys and there shouldn't be much else going on. Please, will you just go along with it? I'll still have you home by curfew."

Sophia looked out the passenger side window. She was still shaking her head in frustration. She put her right elbow on the armrest and rubbed her forehead. The seconds of silence seemed like hours to Andrew. After a few moments Sophia broke the silence, "Ok, I'll do this, but never ask me to do anything like this again. You hear me?"

"Awesome. Thank you, thank you, thank you," Andrew said, breathing a sigh of relief. He reached for his keys to turn the engine back on.

"Oh, and where are going anyway?"

"To the casino," Andrew answered.

"Are you crazy? My parents would never allow this. What are you thinking?"

"Listen, we are not going to gamble or anything like that. There's this magician the guys want to see, and we are only gonna go along with them for the show. I'm a little too young for everything else in there."

Sophia was clearly frustrated, "Andrew, this whole plan keeps getting worse and worse the more you tell me. I hate to think about how this evening is going to end."

Chapter 4

———✦———

Aₙᴅʀᴇw ᴀɴᴅ Sᴏᴘʜɪᴀ ᴀʀʀɪᴠᴇᴅ ᴀᴛ the casino. "I can't believe you are dragging me into this," Sophia said, exiting the truck. Sophia had never been to the Waterloo casino, even though it was a favorite hang out spot in the Waterloo area. Particularly college kids and senior citizens loved it. Located in Northwest Waterloo, the casino prided itself on being "The Family Fun Casino." Of course the gambling was off limits to minors, but there were many amenities for parents and their kids to enjoy. Along with the usual slot machines and tables there was a separate area with a large arcade, a climbing wall, a small bowling alley, and a couple inflatable bouncing areas specifically for young kids. The casino itself was fairly small compared to anything in Vegas, but for Iowa it was considered grand. It consisted of two floors and a grand theater, which frequently hosted musical artists along with other entertainers.

Recently, Charles Chesterton had been performing on a regular basis in the theater. Everyone knew he had come to the Waterloo casino from the outskirts of Reno. There was recently an article written about Chesterton in the local newspaper, further introducing him and his magic act to the public. He was originally from Iowa, but moved out west to pursue his career in stage performance. He was single and always had been. Chesterton was a man of many secrets and he wanted to keep it that way. The biggest controversy surrounding his life was his list of various misdemeanors from years ago. Although he had been clean for the last five or six years, he had quite a lengthy record. When asked about it in the newspaper interview, he just chuckled and said what he always did, responding, "Can't a man just have a little fun?" He never denied his past nor seemed ashamed of it in the least bit.

Approaching the entrance, Andrew reached out and opened the door for Sophia, trying to be a gentleman. She rolled her eyes at him as they passed through the entryway. Entering the casino, there were bright lights everywhere and the bells of slot machines could be heard clearly. From the front entrance, one could also see the climbing wall along with the large inflatable play area where kids were running rapidly. Sophia did not want to be there at all.

Frankie was standing a few feet away from the climbing wall, watching kids ascend. Upon spotting Andrew he quickly jogged over to greet them. "Drew, glad you made it. How ya doin'?"

"I'm doin' fine, thanks," Andrew replied. Even though they'd already met, Andrew was still amazed at Frankie's short but stocky stature. He continued, "Frankie, this is Sophia, a friend of mine."

"Oh, hey, how ya doin'?" Frankie said, extending his hand.

"I'm ok," Sophia replied nonchalantly.

"Just ok, well hey, we are going to have a good time tonight. There's always a party when Johnny and the boys get together," Frankie said with a smile. His New York accent seemed particularly strong tonight.

Sophia shrugged her shoulders, "Yeah, it's just that this is not my thing. Andrew never told me we were heading to the casino."

"Well, here, let me show you guys around. Maybe we can grab a bite to eat or something before the show," Frankie said with a smile. The three of them basically walked around the whole casino twice, waiting for Chesterton's show to begin. Frankie's personality was very welcoming and he could make anyone feel at ease and as if they were a part of his large Italian family. He was very hospitable and never seemed to meet a stranger.

With thirty minutes to go before Chesterton's show, the three of them found a couple chairs outside of the theater where they waited for it to begin. They had met up with Johnny, Dax, and Angela a couple times, but Sophia found the guys to be rude and uncouth. Angela was pleasant, but Sophia disliked her flirtatious and seductive personality.

Twenty minutes before show time, the doors opened and a line started forming. None of the people seemed to be in a real hurry since tickets had to be purchased ahead of time. Johnny, Dax, and Angela arrived at the theater a few minutes later. The two guys were obviously a little buzzed from some of the alcohol they consumed while gambling. Even Angela, who adored Johnny, appeared to be fed up with them. Approaching their friends on the bench, the two guys were laughing hysterically about how much money they lost.

"Fellows, were you able to win back any of the cash?" Frankie asked.

"Ha, don't be silly Frank, we went all in, man. Hey, it's only one life to live. You know what I'm sayin'," Johnny replied, pushing his shaggy hair back behind his ears.

Angela was holding a handful of tickets, "Well, boys, we better get in there and find our seats. This is what I've been waiting for."

The group got into the short line that was moving quickly. Dax, still a little buzzed, reached out and grabbed a strand of Sophia's hair, playing with it. Sophia turned to face him. His height was intimidating to most, but not to Sophia. She quickly brushed his hand aside, giving him an angry look.

"Come on baby, I'm just looking for a little fun. I don't think little Drew here minds sharing you with me," Dax said with a giddy smile. Sophia shook her head with disappointment and disgust. Andrew was ashamed he was not defending her.

"Dax, behave yourself!" Angela warned.

"Cm' on man, you got to treat the ladies with respect," Johnny said, patting his friend on the back.

They passed through the foyer area and entered the dark theater. There was a large curtain at the front covering the stage. The auditorium seemed as if it could hold a couple thousand people. For the last few weeks every show had been sold out. Johnny was able to score some free reserved tickets through a couple friends who worked at the casino.

The group found their seats in the third row, not far from the stage. Dax took his seat in the middle of the row, which was quite problematic with him being 6'5 in height. "Hey, down in front!" someone yelled a few rows back.

"Shut your trap!" Dax said, turning around, challenging the man to a fight. Johnny couldn't help but laugh just a little.

"You just got to let it go, man!" Johnny said, pulling him back down in his seat.

An overhead voice spoke, "Ladies and gentlemen, please quickly find your seats as the show is about to begin."

Andrew turned to face Sophia. He could tell she already wanted to leave. He tried to soften the mood, "Are you having fun yet?" She just rolled her eyes in response. He felt horrible for bringing her into this.

It was just a few moments later that the lights in the theater dimmed further and the curtain began to rise. The audience began to applaud as Charles Chesterton entered the stage. He casually walked to the front of the stage. He was nodding politely at the audience, mouthing the words 'thank you.' He was thin and stood at an average height. He was dressed nicely in a tuxedo along with a top hat. He was sporting a light beard along with his signature eye glasses.

Andrew was fascinated by him. Instantly he could understand Chesterton's popularity. Chesterton carried himself as a man of great mystery. A person wanted to know him, to know who he was, and to know his secrets. Andrew could already tell he was in for a great show.

Chesterton put his hand out softly to quiet the crowd. He smiled and removed his top hat, exposing his thinning brown hair. He looked as if he was preparing to give a lengthy speech. There was a few seconds of silence before he began to speak, "Good evening, ladies and gentlemen! Thank you for coming to my show."

He smiled slightly as he continued, "Every magician has a repertoire of tricks that he regularly performs. These are his favorites and he does not stray from them. You will see many of these tonight. BUT! A magician often becomes complacent and disinterested in his own tricks. He must look for new ways to entertain, not just his audience, but also himself." He paused briefly before continuing, "So without further ado, let us begin, shall we?"

The audience began to clap in anticipation. Chesterton gave a small bow before retreating to the back of the stage in preparation for his first trick. Andrew turned aside, looking at his companions. Johnny seemed unamused by Chesterton's lengthy speech. Angela was resting her head comfortably on his shoulder. Frankie and Sophia seemed interested and were watching intently. Dax, on the other hand, was checking something on his phone, totally disinterested.

Chesterton started his show with the classic Chinese linking rings. He performed the trick flawlessly, linking as many as eight rings together. Andrew found it quite amazing to watch. Even if one knew the secret behind the trick, it would still leave you in wonder as to how it was performed so brilliantly. The audience was locked into every move of the performance.

Chesterton moved very elegantly around the stage. He never missed a step. People often said his performances were like a dance where the audience was led to follow him down a path of mystery and wonder. It wasn't as if his tricks were anything extravagant, but rather *he* was entertaining. Andrew could see even more why Chesterton's show was so very popular.

Chesterton performed many of the classic magic tricks, including pulling multiple rabbits out of his hat and levitating various small objects on the stage. The audience clapped jovially after each trick and laughed at any humor inserted into the performance.

Andrew was relieved to find Sophia enjoying the show. Occasionally she would turn to him in amazement, saying something to the effect of, "how did he do that?" or "wow, did you see that?" Andrew still felt horrible for lying to her and her parents, but at the moment at least he felt a little better, knowing that she was enjoying this part of evening.

The show was heading to a finale. Chesterton had a few simple decks of cards sitting on a table in the middle of the stage. He spun in circles and spoke with humor as he built up the trick. It had been a wonderful show, and Andrew, along with most of the audience were on the edge of their seats, anticipating this grand finale.

Chesterton was casually spinning his top hat in his hand and waving his arms like it was a dance. He was gracefully building up his last trick… when something went terribly wrong. A card! A simple playing card could be seen falling from Chesterton's sleeve. He did not spot it at first, but he could tell something was going wrong by the audience's reaction. They began to murmur. Chesterton quickly looked around to see what the problem was, but it was too late. Not only did one card fall out of his sleeve, but as he went to grab it, a couple more fell out with it. He tried to catch them in the air, but as he did he knocked over the table in the center of the stage. Cards went flying everywhere and the audience could easily tell that some of the cards were attached to others. Turning to catch the table, Chesterton slipped and fell on his face. The audience in the first couple of rows could hear him yell as he hit the ground, "Aww," he moaned in pain.

Nothing like this had ever happened, and the audience was shocked. Chesterton sat up and tried to gather some of the cards. Andrew could hear him speaking under his breath, "What have I done? My trick is ruined. I'm ruined." He looked to be on the verge of crying.

Andrew felt so sorry for Chesterton. He had been executing everything perfectly, without a single flaw. The show had been a beauty to watch. Andrew was looking forward to this finale, and he was sad that Chesterton was not able to cap off his brilliant performance.

After conceding to himself that the trick was ruined and could not be salvaged, Chesterton stood and approached the front of the stage. He picked up his hat that had flown off when he fell. He could not face the audience, but rather stared humbly at the ground. The crowd was silent as they anticipated Chesterton's explanation, or rather, apology.

He spoke, "I'm sorry to end my show that way. I'm sorry you had to witness that ordeal at the end." His voice was shaky, and obviously less certain. "Please forgive me for doing a horrible disservice both to you, the audience, and to the magic community as a whole. I promise to do better in the future, and I will allow all of you to receive a free ticket to a future show of your choosing."

Johnny was shaking his head in laughter. He was not satisfied. He turned to Dax and spoke in a loud voice, "This guy's a joke. Let's get out of here." Everyone in the first few rows heard him, including Chesterton. Chesterton stopped his speech and looked at Johnny. Catching Chesterton's eyes, Johnny stared right back at him. Johnny could see that Chesterton was obviously very displeased by his remarks. Much of the audience was confused by what was transpiring. They could tell that Chesterton was fixated on the college kid in the third row of the theater.

For a few seconds Johnny and Chesterton stared at each other, and it was then that Johnny continued. He spoke a little quieter, but still fixed on Chesterton, "Yeah, you heard me. You're a joke."

Chesterton breathed deeply, trying to calm himself. He closed his eyes. He was obviously upset by Johnny's remarks. After a few seconds he spoke directly to Johnny, "Well, my young viewer, if you would be so kind to stand to your feet for me. Would you please?"

Johnny, never shying away from the limelight, stood to his feet. He was smiling greatly, excited for an opportunity to steal the show. "Thank you," Chesterton continued, "So my young friend, you think I'm a joke, do you?"

Johnny laughed under his breath, "Well, actually you're more like a bad joke that no one wants to hear, but keeps being told." The crowd laughed slightly, impressed by Johnny's confidence.

Chesterton smiled in amusement. He continued, "Well, my friend, may I ask you your name?"

"Johnny, Johnny Platt," he answered confidently.

"Well, Johnny, pleased to meet you," Chesterton, said tipping his hat. He continued, "Well, if we are going to be friends, there are certain things we shouldn't keep from each other."

"Ok, whatever," Johnny said, shaking his head.

"Like for example, may I ask what is in your right pocket?"

"What?" Johnny answered, confused. The audience was following every word.

"You heard me," Chesterton returned, annunciating clearly, "What is in your right pocket?"

Johnny reached into his pocket, confused by the whole ordeal. Searching his pocket, he felt a few items that he could not identify and knew they weren't his. He knew he hadn't put them there. He pulled them out and held them up high in the stage light so he could see what they were. The audience began to whisper to one another and laugh under their breath. One could easily tell that Johnny was holding a large lipstick container along with a woman's pink handkerchief with obvious lace around the border. "What? What is this stuff?" Johnny said to himself. He was truly mystified by the items in his pocket. He looked back up at Chesterton with confusion on his face.

Chesterton smiled and spoke to the crowd, holding out his arms, "Well, I'm often a called a man of secrets, but this young man may have even more secrets than I do." The crowd erupted in laughter and applause as Chesterton smiled and took a large bow to the crowd's ovation. He waved as he walked off the stage. As the curtain began to fall, Johnny threw the lipstick container in anger at the curtain. He had never been so humiliated.

Chapter 5

ANDREW DROVE SOPHIA HOME. IT was dark outside. Neither was talking. Andrew assumed Sophia was still angry that he'd lied to her and then taken her to the casino. He didn't know how he'd ever rectify this situation. His greatest hope was that her parents never found out about them hanging out at the casino.

Andrew glanced at Sophia. She was sitting with her arms crossed. Her facial expression appeared pensive, as if she was thinking deeply about what had just transpired at the theater. There was a sense of wonder and amazement from the evening. Chesterton's tricks were incredible. He wondered if Sophia was replaying some of the tricks in her mind as he had been, trying to unravel the secrets behind them. The urge to see the show again was definitely growing inside him.

The odd ending to the show also left Andrew feeling sorry for both Chesterton and Johnny. The miss on the trick definitely made for an unorthodox ending to a premiere magic show. Chesterton recovered well from his missed trick, but it was to Johnny's embarrassment. Even though this grand trick was not executed, the audience seemed very pleased with the trick aimed at Johnny. Andrew wondered how Chesterton pulled off that trick so quickly, and at the last minute. Johnny seemed both angry and amazed by the feminine items in his pocket. Andrew wondered how Johnny was going to respond.

Andrew broke the silence, "You still mad at me?"

"I am," Sophia responded, nonchalantly.

A few moments of silence passed before Andrew continued on, "I just don't know what to think about that show. I've seen some of those tricks performed by others, but I just don't know how *he* did some of them."

"I feel the same way. I know I've seen Chinese linking rings dozens of times, but this looked more authentic."

"I agree. I wonder if there was something fundamentally different about those tricks, like, I don't know, maybe they weren't done the conventional way," Andrew said, shrugging his shoulders.

It started to rain slightly as they pulled into Sophia's neighborhood. She continued, "It's like there was some deeper level of trickery occurring in that show. I have to admit, I've never seen anything like it before."

They turned onto Sophia's street. Andrew was thankful for the way the mood had been softened. He liked Sophia and hoped that this evening didn't bring any permanent damage to their friendship. After Chesterton's show, she had demanded that he take her home. Andrew wondered if she'd reconsider and hang with the guys back at the college. "Sophia, thanks again for hanging out tonight, and listen, I'm so sorry for lying to you. I definitely should've never done that."

She took her breath and shook her head, "All right, Andrew. Let's just let it go, and please don't do anything like that ever again, ok?"

He felt relief, "Thanks Sophia. I won't do that to you again. I promise."

"I would greatly appreciate that," she said with a slight smile on her face.

Seizing the opportunity, he thought he'd try again to see if she'd hang out with the guys, "Sophia, if you want, the guys are getting together back at Johnny's dorm. I'm sure you're welcome to hang out with us if you want."

"Umm, Andrew, NO!" Sophia said emphatically, "A bunch of college guys in an alcohol infested dorm room doesn't sound like my kind of place. Andrew, I'd watch yourself with those guys. They're nothing but trouble, and besides I imagine Johnny is probably fuming with anger right now."

"Yeah, well, I just thought I'd ask," Drew responded, shrugging his shoulders. He pulled up to her house and stopped the truck.

She opened the door part way and looked over at Andrew. He thought she looked so beautiful in the night under the glow of the street lights. Her blonde hair brushed her shoulders just perfectly as she turned her head. Andrew thought about kissing her. They'd had an emotional evening between the drama of the show and the confessions and apologies in the truck. He thought he would give it a shot. He put his hand on the back of the truck's bench seat. He inched ever so closer to her.

Sophia could tell what was transpiring, "Andrew, are you trying to kiss me?"

"No, no, of course not… I'm just… ummm…"

"Ok, well, have a good night and I'll see you at church tomorrow."

"Good night," he responded.

She opened the door wide and stepped out of the truck. Andrew felt bad he didn't pull into the driveway as there was still a light rain falling. Grabbing the door to close it, she spoke up, "And, Andrew, please be careful around the guys. I've got a feelin' they're going to get you into some trouble."

Andrew looked down at the steering wheel. He knew there was some truth to what she was saying. "Thanks, Sophia, I'll be careful."

"Good-bye," she said, closing the door of the truck and walking toward her house. He watched as she made it safely inside. A part of him wished he was going home as well. Andrew knew Johnny wasn't in a good mood, and he worried a little about Johnny's potential response to the show.

Andrew pulled up to Johnny's dorm hall. He didn't want to be here. It was getting late, already past 11:00 p.m. No matter how late Andrew stayed out, he knew that his dad would wake him just after 8:00 a.m. tomorrow for church. His parents, being very devout Christians, would never allow him to sleep in on Sunday morning. He thought to himself, *I'll just stay out an hour or two and try to sneak out when things calm down.*

Walking up the steps he approached Johnny's dorm. He could hear shouting coming from the room. The urge to leave became stronger. He wanted to turn and go home, but Andrew could almost literally feel the tug of popularity pulling on him. He felt powerless against it. He convinced himself that this is what it took to be in Johnny Platt's inner posse.

Approaching the door, he heard glass shatter as it hit the door. He was taken aback. He hoped there wasn't a fight brewing on the other side of the door. The shouting continued.

He could hear Angela's voice arguing with Johnny, trying to reason with him. *What am I doing here?* Andrew thought to himself. He bit his tongue as he knocked on the door.

The shouting did not stop. He tried again, quickly knocking three times. "Get the door, Frankie!" he heard Johnny say.

Footsteps approached and the door opened swiftly. "Drew!" Frankie announced to the household.

"Hey Frankie, how's going it?"

"Things are a little tense, if you know what I mean," Frankie said in a whisper, cocking his head to the side. Frankie led the way into the living quarters of the dorm room. There was another crash as he approached the others. Johnny was throwing beer bottles, cans, and basically anything he could get his hands on. Johnny's embarrassment at Chesterton's show was greater than Andrew first realized.

Angela was standing to the side trying to talk some sense into him, "Johnny, you can't retaliate during one of his shows. Everyone will know it was you. People know you, Johnny!"

"Did you hear me, Angela? I don't really care one bit. That idiot called me out in front of everyone. No one does that to me and gets away with it," he said, pushing his long shaggy hair out of his face.

She continued, "Johnny, this isn't some college kid that you can play a prank on. This is a business man worth thousands of dollars to the casino. They're not going to let anything to happen to him."

Dax sat comfortably in a chair against the wall. His long gangly limbs made him look like a large spider sprawled out in the chair. "Johnny, let's face it, man, the dude got you and got you good," he said smiling, halfway enjoying the moment.

"Shut up, Dax," Johnny shot back. He turned his gaze toward Andrew, "Drew, come on in. You're going to help me with this." Andrew nervously walked into the living room and took a seat. He thought he could feel Dax roll his eyes.

Angela continued trying to calm the situation. She stepped closer to Johnny, putting her hand on his shoulder, "Listen, Johnny, I would definitely stay away from this guy. I don't think you could handle anything he…"

Johnny quickly turned, pushing her hand off his shoulder. He looked furious, "Shut up, you little witch." She backed away, looking hurt, on the verge of tears.

Frankie decided to throw in his two cents. "Listen, Boss-man," he spoke in his heavy New York accent, "whatever you do, I wouldn't mess with this guy during a show. I think Angela's right. They are going to have security and cameras watching from every angle. It's way too risky, man."

Johnny threw one more bottle against the door before sitting calmly on his sofa. He brushed his blond hair out of his eyes and took a deep breath. A few moments passed and no one said a thing. Johnny patiently sat looking out the window. His mood began to change. Andrew could tell Johnny was contemplating an idea. He was not going to let this go. Johnny was going to find a way to retaliate against Chesterton.

He continued in his normal voice, "Angela, you said Chesterton usually performs on both Saturday and Sunday nights. Does he have a show tomorrow?"

"Yes, he does, but Johnny, like I said, you know we can't do anything during his show. Security will see it coming," she said, frustrated.

Johnny did not react to her frustration. He spoke very articulately, "Well Angela, just like anything I do, I will not confront him head on at first. I will wait, set things up, and then destroy him as best as I know how."

"What are you talking about, Boss?" Frankie asked, puzzled.

"Chesterton is not married and lives alone, correct?" Johnny said, looking over at Angela.

"Yeah, I mean… I think so, but what does this have to do with anything?"

"While he is performing tomorrow we are going to pay a little visit to his house and see his place for ourselves."

"What are you talking about, Johnny?" Angela stood up, startled.

"Listen, you guys are right, we can't just walk into his show and sabotage something. They would see us coming. We are going to hit him where it hurts. Sure, it won't be public, but this will only be the beginning."

Dax nodded his head as he sat comfortably in the chair. It was apparent that he was excited about the idea of breaking into Chesterton's home. He took a sip from a nearby bottle of beer.

Johnny turned toward Andrew, "Drew, do you think you could find where he lives?"

Andrew didn't know what to say. He felt caught in the moment and didn't have time to weigh the consequences of aiding and abetting a crime, "Umm… uhhh… yeah, I could probably find it. I think I saw it on TV a couple weeks ago." He remembered his dad watching a special news segment Channel 7 did on Chesterton from his home.

"Good," Johnny responded, "Frankie, you get all our normal supplies we use for pranks, plus a few bags for carrying away some loot."

"You got it, Boss, whatever you say," Frankie said, shrugging his shoulders.

"Dax, you up for this?"

Dax laughed slightly with a big smile on his face, "Ha, you kiddin' me? I ain't missing this."

"Good," Johnny said, now looking at Andrew, "We are going to need to take your car. I will be a prime suspect for this crime, so I don't want mine anywhere close. People may expect me to retaliate."

Andrew felt his life spinning out of control. He imagined that this would change his life forever. He didn't like the idea of crime, in fact he hated it, but the pull of popularity was strong. He wanted friends. He wanted access into Johnny's inner circle. This would be an instant ticket into college fame. He gave in, "Hey, let's do it, I'm in."

"Awesome. It's all coming together, boys. Chesterton won't know what hit him. This is going to be grand."

Angela seemed beyond frustrated. She stood up, crossing her arms in anger. Andrew thought she looked absolutely gorgeous angry. She spoke up, "Johnny, you just can't do this. I mean... what about the magic?"

"What?" he shot back.

"Listen, you saw the show the other night. I don't know what it is, but there's something different about this guy. You saw those tricks he did. They were unbelievable. We don't know what he's capable of."

"Angela, doll baby," Johnny said, lighting up a cigarette, "This is just some silly middle-aged man we're messing with. It ain't like we never done anything like this before. What are you so afraid of?"

She took a deep breath, "I just don't like this guy, and... his magic kind of scares me."

He calmly blew a little smoke from his mouth, "Well, I'm going to take this opportunity to steal his magic."

Chapter 6

—◦◦◦◦◦◦◦◦◦◦◦—

Andrew was startled as his father opened the door to his bedroom and stuck his head in. "Son, it's time to get up. It's past 8:30 and I gotta be at church early today to help with greeting," he said through his big burly beard.

"Ok, all right Dad, I'll be up shortly," he said pulling the covers back over his head. He felt awful. He had stayed out until about 1:00 a.m. with the guys, finalizing their plans for ransacking Chesterton's house. He was even coerced into drinking a beer before he left Johnny's dorm. It was not sitting well in his stomach this morning.

"Well, Son, please don't make us late," his father said, closing the door.

Andrew stayed in bed just a few more minutes before climbing out. He knew he was going to have to hurry in order to be ready in time. His mind quickly went back to the plans of breaking into Chesterton's home. The thrill and anxiety of it gave Andrew an adrenaline rush. He felt wide awake. Even though Johnny's plans seemed airtight, there was always a fear that something was going to go horribly wrong.

Andrew quickly showered and got ready for the morning. In the kitchen he met his mother who was looking through her purse for her mascara. She was dressed in her Sunday best. There was no time for breakfast, so Andrew quickly grabbed a granola bar. His dad entered the kitchen, fixing his tie. Though dress at their church was a little more casual, Jerry Stevenson always wanted them to look their best for the Sunday service, especially since Jerry was the head deacon. "You guys ready to go?" he said calmly.

Andrew wondered why it was only the three of them. "Hey, where's Elliot? Why isn't he with us?"

"Oh," his mother turned to look at him, "he's not feeling well today. I think he feels a little nauseated from his broken nose and all."

Andrew had completely forgotten about the incident with his brother. His mind had been focused solely on Johnny and the guys. "Oh, well, hopefully it's not too bad," he responded. Though he still felt justified for punching his brother, he did hope that Elliot recovered soon. He wanted his brother to help him fix his car, and Andrew wanted him to know the full extent of the damage he had caused.

For the most part it was a typical morning at church. Andrew was only mildly interested in the college-age Sunday school class. He'd heard it all before, the Devil is the thief that comes to steal, kill, and destroy, but Jesus came to give us life, and not just an ordinary life, but life to the fullest. The challenge was the same as he'd heard last time, "Choose the abundant life

Jesus has for you." *Blah, blah, blah,* Andrew thought to himself. He'd understood it the first time. Sure, he believed it all, but he felt he was doing all right. He was a pretty good guy. He didn't feel like he needed this every Sunday.

The pastor's message was even worse. It was about forgiveness. "Jesus has forgiven us so much. Let us embrace Him and forgive others as we have been forgiven," the pastor said in his closing remarks. Once again, a topic he had heard all his life in church. *Sure, we need to ask God's forgiveness for our sins. I already did that a long time ago,* Andrew thought. Sitting through two messages every Sunday was something that was starting to get old and getting old fast.

The only highlight of the morning was seeing Sophia after the preaching service. Andrew spotted her coming out of the sanctuary. "Sophia!" Andrew yelled, walking over to where she stood.

"Oh hey," she said, a little surprised.

"How's it going?"

"It's going ok, I'm just glad to be here this morning after last night."

"Yeah, I know what you mean. That got awkward really fast," Andrew said, scratching the back of his head. He chose his words carefully, "Johnny was pretty upset when he got to the dorm room. It wasn't a pretty sight."

"Well that's too bad," Sophia said, brushing her long blonde hair to the side, "but a part of me says this serves him right. It was probably a good thing that someone had the guts to stand up to him. I hope he learned a lesson."

Sophia's statement caught Andrew off guard. He turned to look out a window. He couldn't face her. Sophia could tell Andrew was contemplating something, "Andrew, what's going on?"

"What do you mean?" he responded, looking right at her.

"You know what I mean. Johnny is up to something, isn't he?"

"I don't know…I mean, maybe," Andrew said, trying to look away.

She grabbed his arm and pulled him aside from the flow of people coming from the sanctuary. She spoke intently, "Andrew, whatever it is he has planned, you can't get involved. These guys are headed for trouble. You need to get away from them."

"They're my friends. Sophia, listen, nothing will happen to me. Johnny's never been caught doing a prank and I think he's…"

"Andrew, stop it," Sophia spoke in a strong whisper. The expression on her face was a mixture of sadness and frustration. "You can't be getting involved here. These guys are leading you into trouble."

Already Andrew was ready for this conversation to be over. "Sophia, just don't worry about me. We are just going to play a little prank on Chesterton and everything will be all right."

"Andrew," Sophia looked at her feet, trying to choose her words carefully, "I wouldn't mess with that man. I think there's more to him than what we are seeing. It's like he's clouded with mystery or something.

"He's a magician, what do you expect?" Andrew shot back.

"Andrew, just…please be careful, ok?"

"Sure," he said shrugging it off. He didn't even want to think about what Sophia was saying. He knew she was at least partly correct.

He was about to walk away when she continued, "Oh, and Andrew, my parents didn't find out about last night. If we could, let's keep it between you and me if that's all right. I can't imagine what they would do if they found out I went to a casino."

Andrew smiled, "You got it! Not a word from me." Sophia smiled as she walked away. Andrew looked at her admiringly. He thought she always looked her best on Sunday mornings. Though the night before had been awkward, his attraction for her was growing. He was happy to find out that her parents did not know about the magic show, or even going to the casino for that matter. Andrew was thankful that they were so trusting of him, but a part of him did feel ashamed for putting Sophia in that type of situation. He cared for Sophia and didn't want anything to happen to her.

The Stevensons were the last people to leave the church. Andrew's dad had to stay and lock up after everyone left. Andrew was frustrated it took them so long to leave.

Arriving back at home after church, his mother ran straight to Elliot's room to check on him. Andrew's mind instantly went back to the plans for the evening. He had never done anything like this before, but he trusted Johnny enough to know that he could orchestrate a good enough plan to keep them from getting caught. Andrew was excited for the college fame and popularity this would bring him.

Andrew walked over to the fridge and began looking for food. "Dad, do you know what we're doing for lunch? It doesn't look like mom has anything prepared."

His dad was loosening his tie. "Son, I don't think your mother has had time to plan anything. You know how busy she has been lately, helping your Grandma and all. We may have to order some pizza or something of that sort."

Shutting the refrigerator, Andrew grabbed the phone book and started looking through the Yellow Pages for a pizza place. "Where do you want to get it, Dad?"

"Anywhere's fine," his dad responded, relaxing comfortably in a recliner. He was always easy to please.

The house seemed strangely quiet, when Andrew heard his mother yell out, "Jerry, come quick!" Andrew's dad jumped out of the chair and ran toward his wife. She was still in Elliot's room. Andrew followed his dad down the hall, and entered the room right after him.

He found his mother sitting on the edge of the bed, cradling Elliot's head in her lap. The expression on her face was a mixture of sadness and panic. "Jerry, something's not right. He seems barely conscious and his nose is swelling and looks awful. We need to get him to the doctor, now!"

His father agreed and quickly picked him up in his arms. Elliot's body was no problem for Andrew's 6'4, 275 lb. father. He held Elliot easily in his arms. In a hurry, Andrew's mom ran out of the room to grab her purse. She was in a near panic. Andrew's father was more calm. He never seemed to get very excited and he was always steady under pressure.

Andrew just stood and watched. He thought his mom was very much overreacting. Elliot's nose was probably broken and this was most likely the normal healing process for it. *Everything's going to be fine*, he thought, *just give him a little time and he'll be right back to his old self.* He retreated back to the living room to continue looking for the right pizza place.

Andrew's parents walked past him on the way out the door. His dad was still carrying Elliot in his arms. Elliot was moaning and squirming a little, as if he was trying to get comfortable. He was obviously in pain. Before going out the door, Andrew's mom turned to him for a couple of parting instructions. "We're heading up to the hospital. I'm not sure how long we will be," she was speaking very quickly, looking intently at Andrew as she spoke, "I'll give Grandma a call to come over and check on you if things get too late.

Andrew wanted to roll his eyes. He was old enough to take care of himself. Even though he loved her, he didn't need his grandmother checking on him. "All right, I'll be fine, Mom. You just…take care of Elliot," he said, trying to ease his mother's fear just a little.

"Thanks, Andrew. I'll let you know if we hear anything."

"Thanks, Mom," Andrew said. His parents left right away through the garage. They were taking his mother's car. Andrew could hear the sound of the garage door opening and shutting, along with his parents pulling out and driving away. With that the house was quiet. Andrew imagined that their stay at the hospital would be short. Elliot would probably be x-rayed, given a couple pills, and then released. On second thought, Andrew imagined his brother probably just got dehydrated or light-headed from his blood loss yesterday. *Everything's going to be fine,* he thought to himself.

He reached for his phone along with the Yellow Pages. Picking up his phone he noticed that he had missed a call from Johnny. His mind instantly went back to the task at hand, breaking into Chesterton's home. He quickly checked his voicemail, "Drew, what's up? I'm going to need you over here with your wheels as soon as you can," Johnny sounded relaxed on the message. "We need to iron out a few last minute details before we pull this off. Go ahead and make sure your car has enough gas for tonight before you head over here. We can't be seen after we're in gear. All right, we'll see you, man."

Andrew put the phone down. He wasn't hungry anymore. The reality of the situation hit him hard in that moment. He started to sweat thinking about the crime. Sophia's admonitions became more real; *what if I get caught?* he thought. He knew that his whole academic career was possibly on the line. Not only that, he knew he was looking at a possible felony or maybe even some jail time if they were caught. Andrew had to sit down from all the stress.

The only thing that comforted him was Johnny's confidence. He kept telling himself that Johnny had done this a hundred times and had never been caught. This was not going to be the first time.

Chapter 7

———— ·VWV-o-Q~~~O~~Q-o-o-VW· ————

Andrew sat in the back seat of his car. This was a very awkward situation for him; he had never ridden in the back seat of his own car before. Johnny was driving, with Dax in the passenger seat. Frankie was beside Andrew. All four were dressed completely in black, including thin black gloves. They even had dark ski masks they would put on as they got closer to Chesterton's property. Looking down at the mask in his hands, Andrew wondered how he got here. Sophia's final warning kept ringing in his ears.

Chesterton's home was a fairly easy place to find. It was located in southeast Waterloo, just on the edge of town. Johnny had devised a plan that seemed flawless. He had everything nailed down, including when Chesterton would take the stage at the casino and when he might arrive back at his home. Of course Johnny figured they would be long gone before Chesterton ever thought about returning home.

The current time was 8:35 p.m. Johnny planned for them to be in the house about 9:00, and to be out by 9:30 on the dot. He knew how they were to enter and exit, and exactly how they were going to execute this plan. Chesterton took the stage at 9:00 p.m. at the casino, so there should be no worry about him returning home prematurely.

They were just a few minutes away when Johnny reminded them of their initial steps, "Frankie, I'm going to need you to take the wheel after we arrive near the back of his property. We'll make our way through the woods and enter on the east side. Remember, you're going to park the car at the small city park just a couple blocks up the road. There's a trail through the woods that will take you near the front of his property. Once you arrive, go around back, and shoot me a text when you make it to the back gate and we'll just let you in."

"Sounds good, Boss," Frankie said, nodding his head in agreement.

"Drew, remember when you get in the house look for anything sentimental that we could possibly use to bribe him or prank him later in the week; anything that would let us know who this guy really is."

"Ok," Andrew said, his voice cracking just a little.

"Frankie, once you arrive, remember to keep a hard look out for anything suspicious that might be coming our way."

"You got it," Frankie said, expressing his full allegiance.

Johnny continued, "Dax, take whatever you can find that's valuable: gold, jewelry, anything of that sort. Nothing too large."

"Yeah, I got it, man. I know what I'm doing," Dax responded, "What are you going to do, Johnny?"

"I'm going to steal his magic. I'm going to look for anything that will tell me how he does his tricks. I'm going to use his secrets and duplicate them or at least use them to sabotage his show."

Dax smiled as he spoke, "I think you really just want to know how he put all that girly stuff in your pocket."

Johnny shook his head angrily, remembering the incident, "That will be the last trick he ever plays on me."

Chesterton sat comfortably in a back room behind the stage. It was just a few minutes before show time. He was casually shuffling through a deck of cards, just keeping his hands busy. He was anxious to get back on stage. The debacle at the end of last night's show made him anxious to get it right this time. His card multiplicity trick was a finale truly worthy of his show. He couldn't wait to perform it and get it right this time.

So far things were turning out well in Iowa. He was glad to be back, at least for a time. Sure, there was less glamour and fame in a small Iowa casino, but he didn't care. He wanted the opportunity to try out new tricks without the constant pressure from the Nevada media and magic community. The Waterloo Casino had proven so far to be a perfect place to get back to the real reason he loved magic.

Chesterton's mind went back to the blond-headed college kid he tricked at the end of last night's show. It brought a smile to his face. That kid seemed truly caught off guard by the trick he pulled at the close of the show. It proved to be somewhat adequate for a show's finale. The look on the kid's face was perfect, and the laughter from the audience was 'oh, so sweet.'

He heard a knock on the door. "Come in," he responded. It was his beautiful assistant. He had brought her with him from his Reno show. It was great to have her back on stage with him tonight. Chesterton thought she looked absolutely gorgeous in her red stage outfit. She was also wearing lots of make-up. A beautiful woman in a magic show is one of the best distractions a magician can have.

"Show's in five minutes, Charles," she said, giving him a small smile and wink.

"Thanks, Love," Chesterton responded. He put the cards back into a stack, holding the deck in the palm of his hand. He could tell by the weight of the cards that one was missing. He knew his deck that well. These were his custom made silver-plated cards. They dazzled and sparkled brilliantly on stage. This particular night they were going to be the key to his trick.

He quickly stuffed a couple other decks of cards in his pocket. "Let the show begin," Chesterton whispered to himself.

Frankie pulled up to a wooded area behind Chesterton's home. They were about a quarter mile from his property. Johnny didn't want to be seen close to the home. The boys quickly got out and shut their doors as quietly as they could. Frankie quickly drove away. There were no other cars close by. Things seemed very quiet. It appeared to be a perfect night for a robbery.

They approached the woods and ducked behind a clump of trees. Johnny put on his ski mask. Andrew and Dax followed suit. Johnny and Dax both had a few miscellaneous items they thought they would need once inside the home. Dax, in fact, was carrying a small black duffle bag, into which he would collect some of Chesterton's valuables. "Let's go, boys," Johnny whispered, sneaking off in the direction of Chesterton's home.

They instantly began moving at a brisk pace. Andrew couldn't believe how comfortable Johnny seemed, knowing they were about to break into a man's home. He followed behind both guys, a few feet behind, "Keep up, you pansy,"

Dax whispered back to him. Andrew felt himself shaking as he trotted through the woods. He was sweating and he even felt his eyes welling up with tears. *How did I get here*, he asked himself. All the emotions of the situation overwhelmed him. He even felt a little remorse. His parents had raised him better than this. He thought of his father who worked hard for the family and always encouraged him to stay on the straight and narrow. He thought of Sophia and others at his church who were always supportive of him. If an opportunity to get away had arisen at that moment, he would have done so. But in reality he knew that any attempt to break from the plan would have resulted in terrible retribution from Johnny and Dax. Leaving was not an option.

As they approached the outside fence Andrew could see a few faint lights from Chesterton's home. The fence was more like a solid white wall that stood approximately seven feet in height. It was very intimidating to behold. Johnny went to work inspecting the outside base of the wall. He was clearly looking for something. "Johnny, what are you looking for?" Andrew asked, trembling as he spoke.

"A lot of large homes like this have their security lines running a couple feet underground to an outside power source. If you know what you are looking for, it's a simple find and a simple cut."

Dax took a seat beside a nearby tree, thinking they were going to be a while.

"Aw, here we go," Johnny spoke quietly. He removed a small garden shovel from Dax's duffle bag and began digging. He was careful not to throw dirt too far because he would want to bury the line again after it was cut. After a couple minutes, Johnny pulled up a large electrical line. Dax pulled a pair of hedge shears from his duffle bag. The line was quite thick, but Johnny was able to get it cut. Step one was complete. "All right, let's do it boys," Johnny stated. "Andrew, you first," he whispered.

Andrew was on autopilot at this point. Johnny and Dax got down on one knee and cupped their hands. They were going to lift Andrew over first. He put his hands on their shoulders and his foot in their hands. They quickly lifted him up. Andrew grabbed the top of the wall and with one quick motion, threw himself over. His fall was not pleasant. He fell on a bush planted at the base of the wall. One of its branches stuck him right in the ribs. He could see that it cut a little hole in his black shirt.

Gathering himself, he took in the full sight of Chesterton's home. It was a beautiful white mansion, at least two stories. Anyone who saw it would instantly know that a person of fame or great wealth lived there. There was a beautiful fountain in front and Andrew could see the edge of a swimming pool in the back. There were a few old style lampposts along the long driveway that were giving off a small amount of light.

Johnny came over the wall, landing on his feet. Next, Dax's duffle bag came flying over, just a few feet from where they were standing. Dax himself followed a few seconds later. Thankfully, Dax was tall enough that he didn't need a hand getting over the wall.

Johnny walked confidently toward Chesterton's home without fear of being seen. As they approached the home Johnny turned to Andrew. "Drew, Frankie's already at the back gate, go let him in!" he said firmly. Andrew was amazed Frankie had made it to the gate so fast.

Without responding Andrew veered from the guys and approached the back gate. There was a long driveway lit by a few lampposts that led from the house to the gate. Andrew stayed back in the shadows. Frankie was crouching behind a bush beside the gate. Andrew wondered how he was going to get it open. He whispered to Frankie as he got close, "Frankie, how do I get this gate open?"

"I've seen this type of gate before. There should be a manual release somewhere on the inside," Frankie responded. Looking up the gate about six and a half feet from the ground, Andrew found the lever. He stretched for it, standing on his tiptoes. Pulling the lever, he felt the tension in the doors release. Frankie quickly stood to his feet, pushing the gate in. Andrew wasn't able to get out of the way, and a metal hook on the gate snagged a piece of his sleeve, tearing the fabric, along with the skin underneath. "Aww!" he yelled. It was deep. He knew a few stitches may be required. He quickly grabbed his right forearm, trying to stop the flow of blood.

"Drew, you ok?" Frankie asked, his New York accent seemed to be stronger when he whispered.

"Yeah, I'm fine, let's just get inside," Andrew said, not wanting to take any chance of being seen outside of Chesterton's home. Even though the cut was deep, Andrew's pain was minimal; his adrenaline was going strong.

The two boys quickly ran toward the house. Andrew could see that Johnny had left a side door cracked for them. Frankie quietly opened the door just wide enough for the two of them to enter.

The inside of Chesterton's home was as beautiful as the outside. It was marvelously decorated, having the décor of both a twenty-first century penthouse and a quiet Iowa home. They had entered at a quiet sunroom that was beautifully tiled. Andrew could see the living room to his left with the kitchen and dining room to his right. The kitchen looked beautifully furnished and would be the envy of any cook. He could see a high end mixer and coffee maker, an extravagant spice rack, and a large wine cabinet, among other things. The dining room table looked to be made of solid wood. It looked quite prestigious. Looking toward the living room he could see it was also wonderfully decorated. It had elegant couches, rustic lamps and large clay vases on the coffee tables. A huge flat screen TV seemed to be the focal point of the room. Andrew noticed small speakers situated around the room. They appeared to be connected to a large stereo system by the television. The room was truly a bachelor's dream.

Frankie positioned himself by a large open window by the dining room table. He truly had a good position to see if anyone was coming. Andrew was stunned for a moment trying to take in everything. It was a wonderful home.

Johnny was currently looking through various drawers in the living room. He had a flashlight in hand. Seeing Drew frozen by the door, he tried to snap him out of it, "Drew, get to work, man, we don't have much time. Check upstairs, see if there is anything we can snag up there."

Andrew gathered himself and approached the stairwell on the other side of the living room. There were beautiful rugs positioned in high trafficked areas on the wood floors. Even though he was an intruder, a part of him felt badly about stepping on them with dirty shoes. He had to step around Dax who was unplugging a couple speakers on a nearby coffee table.

Reaching the stairs, Andrew tried to ascend quietly. Each step seemed to creak as he placed his foot down. He felt as if every sound in the steps was a trumpet blast. There was a gorgeous wooden banister along the side. Andrew used it to ease his steps. On the walls he noticed paintings of various European scenes. Many of them looked to be scenes of Venice or Paris. Something about them was intimidating to look at.

Reaching the top of the stairwell, Andrew noticed about four rooms upstairs. He saw two rooms to his left. Stepping closer to one doorway, he peeked inside. Seeing that it was just the upstairs bathroom, he decided to move on. He moved on to the room farthest to his left. The door was completely shut. He turned the handle and opened the door. He could tell right away it was Chesterton's bedroom.

The room was simply laid out with a king-sized bed in the middle of the room, along with a small dresser. The bed was made and everything seemed to be in order. At the far end of the room were two double doors that opened out onto a balcony. The room was dark but there was just enough light coming from the outside for him to see.

He stepped further into the room. The room seemed quiet, *possibly a little too quiet*, Andrew thought. He walked closer to the dresser, thinking he would find something of value located in it.

Stepping closer to it, he noticed a single ring sitting in the middle of it. It looked like an old high school or maybe a college ring of some sort. It was gold, but well worn. Years of wear had obviously gotten to it. He tried to read the markings on the side, but they were a little too faded to make out the exact wording.

Picking it up and examining it closely, he thought the ring looked very familiar. It was very similar to one he had seen before. In fact he wondered if he had seen this ring before. Possibly the anxiety of the situation was getting to him. He felt as if he was having a strange case of déjà vu.

Looking up from the dresser, Andrew gasped and just about fell backwards. He was startled and let out a small shout. Thinking he'd seen someone, he quickly realized it was only his reflection in the dresser mirror. With the tension and fear he already felt, the simple sight of himself in dark clothes and a ski mask had spooked him. He breathed deeply to catch his breath.

Realizing he still had the ring in his hand, he quickly stuffed it in his pocket and left the room in a hurry. He continued to hold tight to his arm. Blood was starting to soak through the sleeve of his shirt. He tried not to focus on his cut; it only made him light headed.

Entering the hallway again, he could hear someone rummaging through one of the rooms on the opposite end. He slowly walked over. He was still breathing heavily and was a little on edge from the scare in the mirror. Everything seemed to be amplified at the moment. His breathing felt like shouts, and every creak in the floor sounded like a large crack. Andrew tried hard to calm himself.

Slowly peeking into the far room, he could see someone looking through various papers and contraptions. It was Johnny. He had his mask off and was shining his flashlight as he looked.

The room was obviously Chesterton's "magic room." It was where he designed his tricks and kept his secret files on them. The room was no larger than an average bedroom, but it was completely packed full. Andrew saw small devices such as linking rings and top hats, along with large items such as cages and decorative boxes big enough to fit a small person inside. Andrew even spotted a rabbit in a cage on the far end of the room. He entered the room to get a better look.

Johnny glanced at Andrew as he entered, "Drew, how's it going? Did you find anything?"

"No, not really," Andrew replied, not wanting to mention the ring. His odd familiarity with it made him want to keep it a secret from Johnny.

"I'm looking through his secrets. Most of the engineering for his tricks is all right here, written out on these papers. It seems like he was constantly trying to develop new tricks."

Andrew walked over and looked at some of the papers Johnny was rummaging through. Some were just brief sketches, while others were extensive layouts of where and how tricks were going to be performed. It all looked fascinating. In a different situation Andrew would have loved to read through these papers for hours. He would have enjoyed learning the mechanics of how the tricks were done.

Johnny checked his watch. "Drew, I'm 'bout ready to get out of here. Stuff some of these papers into your pocket. I'm going to see if I can carry out a few of his simple contraptions." Andrew grabbed a handful of papers, probably around thirty in all. He folded them up as best as he could and stuffed them into his pocket. Johnny quickly walked around the room and grabbed whatever he could hold.

Glancing around the room, Andrew noticed something on the floor. It was just a few feet from the door. It was small but shiny. He stepped closer to have a look. Crouching over it, he noticed it was the size of a playing card. Picking it up, he realized it was a playing card, the Ace of Hearts. The backside of the card looked to be silver plated. Its design was a beautiful interwoven flower pattern. It was unlike any playing card Andrew had ever seen. He knew right away that this card had some sort of special purpose for one of Chesterton's tricks. He was mesmerized by it.

Andrew was caught up in the wonder of the card when Johnny got his attention. "Drew, let's get out of here, man. I've got everything I need."

Andrew carefully wrapped the card in one of the folded papers and put it back into his pocket. He didn't want anything to happen to this card. The beauty of it made it look like a piece of artwork in and of itself. He couldn't imagine seeing a whole deck of them. He hoped it would stay in good condition until he got back home.

Exiting the room, the boys quickly descended the steps. Dax was still in the living room, but at this time he appeared to be just vandalizing Chesterton's home, pulling down various pictures on the wall, and smashing any electronic equipment he could find. Andrew felt sad seeing such a beautiful home vandalized. In fact Andrew really loved and appreciated this house. It was a very comfortable home, but also full of mystery. Even though he was fearful of being there, a part of him wanted to stay longer and explore more of the house. He felt as if they had only scratched the surface.

Hearing the guys come down the steps, Frankie ran over to greet them, obviously shaking, "Fellows, I think we should get out of here. There's something in this house that I just don't like." Panic was evident in his voice.

"Frankie, chill out, man. You're starting to sound superstitious," Johnny said, trying to keep him calm. "Dax, you had enough man?"

"Almost!" he responded, looking around for something. He saw a little vase sitting on an end table near the couch. Walking over to it, Dax picked it up and with one quick motion he threw it hard at Chesterton's flat screen TV, mounted on the wall. It hit hard. The TV came down with a crash, breaking the glass table under it, and smashing the screen. Andrew covered his eyes, fearing some glass may ricochet.

It happened so quickly, and in a matter of moments everything was quiet again. Johnny gave a slight smile, "That'll do Dax, let's get out of here."

All four boys approached the side door they came in. Frankie exited first, anxiously ready to leave Chesterton's home. Dax and Johnny followed. "Drew, be sure to close the door on your way out," Johnny said sarcastically.

Reaching for the door handle, Andrew's right arm rubbed against the side of the door, leaving a small mark of blood on it. Not wanting anyone to see it, he quickly tried to wipe it off. Great fear was settling in his mind. He thought if the police found this stain on the door, they could easily trace it back to him. He started to sweat and panic, frantically trying to wipe it off. But the more he tried, the more it seemed to smear and stain the door.

"Drew, let's go!" Johnny shouted back. Not wanting to tell Johnny about the blood, he quickly shut the door and ran to catch up with the guys who were approaching the back gate.

"God, help me!" Andrew prayed as he ran after the guys.

Chapter 8

THE SUN SHONE THROUGH THE window in his bedroom. Andrew stumbled out of bed. He felt awful. Last night's robbery left him with shame and many regrets. He couldn't believe he'd broken into someone's home. It seemed like some strange dream.

After arriving back at the car last night, Andrew dropped the guys off at the university and headed home. He had arrived back at his house just after 10:00 p.m. Johnny thought they ought to go ahead and disperse for the evening so they wouldn't be seen together. Andrew had tried to go to bed early, but he found himself lying wide awake in bed for a few hours, unable to sleep. He didn't feel well rested this morning.

Even though it was Monday morning and Andrew had a few assignments due, he had decided that he was not going to class today. He had too much anxiety from the night before, and he had a strong headache because of it. He was so scared they were going to get caught. He wondered if news of the robbery would be in the paper or on the local news.

Andrew headed toward the bathroom. He had wrapped his forearm again when he arrived back at his house. Upon seeing it this morning, the blood had soaked through the cream-colored bandage. He knew that he would have to rewrap it.

Once in the bathroom, he slowly unwrapped his arm. He found that the cut was deeper and longer than he remembered. He knew beyond a shadow of a doubt that he would need stitches. The cut was about three inches long and was still slightly bleeding. He knew that it was too deep to put rubbing alcohol or peroxide on it. Turning on the cold water, he washed it one more time. Andrew wondered how he was ever going to hide this from his parents. He didn't want anyone to find out about it for at least a few days.

After rewrapping his arm, he quickly went back to his room and put on a long sleeved shirt to hide the cut. It was just past 8:00 a.m. and he figured his dad was at work by now. He headed to the kitchen for breakfast. He didn't want to see anyone.

Entering the kitchen, he grabbed a bowl from the cabinet. He looked at his cereal options. He hadn't eaten anything since yesterday's breakfast. He was practically starving.

Andrew heard someone coming. He pivoted himself to hide his right arm from being seen. Even though it was covered up, he couldn't take the risk of any blood soaking through his sleeve and being seen. He tried to look casual.

His mother came into view. She was dressed professionally with her purse in hand and looked ready to head out the door. She seemed to be in a hurry. No one was home when he arrived home last night. They were still at the hospital with Elliot. Seeing Andrew, she spoke up, "Andrew, why are you still here? Shouldn't you be on your way to school?"

"Yeah, I'm not feeling well today, so I thought I'd take the day off. Not much is going on anyway."

"Ok, well don't do this too much," Diane said firmly, "We're paying for this education and we don't want to see it go to waste."

"Right, Mom," Andrew said, rolling his eyes slightly.

"Ok, well look, I'm heading back up to the hospital, your dad stayed the night and…"

"Wait, what?" Andrew said, interrupting his mother.

"I left a message on your phone, didn't you get it?"

"No, I guess…I wasn't looking, or something," Andrew said, stuttering over his words.

"Listen, your brother has a slight infection in his nose, and the doctors wanted to keep him overnight, just to see how he responded to the antibiotics. Hopefully things will be a lot better today," Diane said, heading toward the door.

So many questions flooded Andrew's mind, "Whoa! Well, where's Dad? Did he come home last night?"

"No. Like I said, your father stayed the night in the hospital, and he's still there with your brother. He just couldn't leave him alone, and…" She stopped midsentence and Andrew could see she was stunned. "Andrew, what in the world happened to you?"

Andrew looked down at his arm at the first reaction. He didn't see any blood coming through his sleeve and everything looked fine. Looking back at his mother, he saw that she was looking at his right pant leg. Looking down, he saw that it was covered in dried blood. This morning he hadn't bothered to look at his pants, but it appeared that his arm had rested against his leg for a portion of the night. The blood had soaked through his bandages and stained his pant leg, rather heavily too. He was speechless.

His mother continued, "Andrew, you tell me right now, what is going on? And I want the truth!"

"Ah, Mom, it's all right. I just got a little cut last night when I was with the guys. It's no big deal. I'll be fine."

"Andrew Stevenson, you let me see the cut right now," his mom said in a panic. Andrew thought his mom seemed overly anxious. He figured that all the worry concerning Elliot had left her on edge.

"Oh, Mom, you shouldn't worry about it. I just had…"

"Andrew!" she said, holding her index finger in front of her mouth to silence him. She was angry at this point. "Let me see your cut," she said firmly.

Breathing deeply, Andrew pulled back his right sleeve exposing his wrapped arm. He rolled his eyes as he began to meticulously unroll the wrapping. His arm stung with pain as he pulled the wrapping from his skin. Exposing the cut, his mom froze with horror, covering her mouth with her hand.

Andrew tried to calm her, "It's not that bad really. I think it maybe looks worse than it really is."

"That's deep," she said, gently grabbing his arm and pulling it closer to her eyes. "We've got to get you to the emergency room right now." That was the last place Andrew wanted to be at that moment.

"Mom, I'm fine," he said, pulling his arm away. "Listen, let's just give it some time and I think it will heal up on its own."

"Honey, you're going to the hospital with me right now, and this is not up for discussion," his mother said, looking him squarely in the eyes. Andrew knew there was no point in arguing any longer.

They arrived at the emergency room of the hospital. There were only a couple people sitting and waiting. Diane hadn't given her son any time to shower or eat breakfast. She knew the severity of the cut and that it had to be taken care of right away. Normally, Andrew would have felt embarrassed going anywhere without showering or "fixing" his hair, but today his only worry was making sure no one found out how he really cut his arm. He wore a green Eastern Iowa hat to cover his face.

Diane walked up to the front desk to check him in. Andrew stood at her side, listening to her answer all the necessary questions. He noticed a TV to his left. The local morning news was on. He watched it closely, trying to see if there would be anything concerning the robbery of Chesterton's home. There were headlines running across the bottom of the screen. He read them breathlessly as they slowly scrolled. So far, he saw nothing about a robbery or about Chesterton himself.

His mom interrupted his train of thought, "Come on, Andrew," she said directing him toward the waiting area. They waited for what seemed like hours to Andrew, but in reality it was only about twenty minutes. He kept watching the same news stories cycle through over and over again. He tried to keep conversation with his mother at a minimum. He didn't want to answer many questions about how he actually got the cut on his arm. His answers would create a web of lies.

Eventually Andrew's name was called and he was led to a standard patient room. Once he was settled his mom said she was going to quickly go check on Elliot, who was at the other end of the hospital. "I'll be back shortly," she assured him as she left.

A young female nurse arrived just shortly after his mother left. "Hello," she said, pleasantly smiling as she entered the room. She was short and attractive and looked to be in her mid-twenties.

"Hey," Andrew responded. All of sudden he became aware that his hygiene was subpar this morning. He hadn't even had time to brush his teeth.

"Well, I'm just here to get some initial blood work and see if I can clean things up a little bit before the doctor comes in."

"Sounds good," Andrew said, trying to look away as he spoke. He didn't want the young nurse exposed to his morning breath.

She put on a set of gloves and stepped closer to Andrew. "Ok, well let's see what we have here," she said, twisting his arm slightly to get a good look at the cut. The nurse continued, "And how did you say you got this?"

"Oh, I cut it on a gate…umm… at the school, the university that is."

She looked puzzled, "A gate at the school? At Eastern Iowa, or UNI?"

"At Eastern, that's where I go."

"What gate are you talking about? I just graduated from there last spring."

Andrew felt caught, he didn't know where to go with this, "Yeah, you see, the school is trying this new thing with the dorm buildings where you enter through a gate you get in." He was making it up as he went, "The gate swung open and caught my arm, and, uh… that's how I got this cut."

The nurse just shook her head as she went to get a few cleaning pads. Her mood seemed to change. She spoke disappointedly as she cleaned his cut, "Andrew, you need to be careful with yourself; a lot of kids at Eastern Iowa mess themselves up with alcohol or drugs. From a graduate to a student I would caution you, please be careful."

Andrew nodded his head in agreement. He didn't know what to say. Though she was wrong in her conclusion, she knew he was lying. He felt ashamed and embarrassed that he had lied to this beautiful young nurse. He was quiet as she thoroughly cleaned his cut and then took his blood pressure. "The doctor will be in shortly," she said, leaving the room.

"Thanks," Andrew replied, grateful but very much disappointed with himself. He knew that he was going to have to lie over and over again in order to cover his tracks. The worst part was that he would he have to continue this, not just with doctors and nurses, but with family as well.

It was just a few minutes later that the nurse came back through the door. "Hey," she said, looking a little puzzled.

"Hello," Andrew responded, wondering if everything was ok.

She was holding an enveloped note in her hand. "Some man out there told me to give you this note."

"Thanks," Andrew said, grabbing it. He looked it over. It was a small envelope, of the standard 'thank-you' note variety. The front of the card simply said 'Andrew,' written in very neat cursive handwriting. He wondered where it came from.

"The doctor should be in soon," the nurse said, leaving the room.

Andrew studied the envelope carefully before turning it over. It felt thick, and the card itself was almost a perfect square. The seal on the flap broke easily. He slowly pulled out the card. The outside was completely blank. Opening it up, he saw that the card was addressed to him and there were just a couple of sentences written:

Andrew,

How exactly did you get that cut on your arm? I'm watching you!

Yours truly,
Mr. Chesterton

Andrew dropped the card and quickly jumped off the exam table. He felt afraid. He had no idea what he should do. Chesterton could be anywhere and he was stuck inside this hospital room. He began to pace back and forth across the room. He wanted to get out of there. He ran toward the door but was stopped as someone was entering the room.

It was the doctor. He was dressed in a long white lab coat and looked very much like a stereotypical doctor. He had a light beard with slightly thinning brown hair. Instantly Andrew thought the doctor looked remarkably similar to Chesterton. He wondered if it was Chesterton. He backed away from the door. Not seeing a chair behind him, he tripped over it, falling backward. His head hit a counter as he fell hard to the ground. Andrew was knocked out cold.

Chapter 9

—⌘—

Johnny walked through the campus of Eastern Iowa University. It was late in the evening. He had four classes on Thursday and he rarely went to all of them. He was happy they were over. Andrew had not been in class today to cheat off of. He was still not himself after thinking he saw Chesterton at the hospital. He ended up falling and receiving a small concussion. Johnny had spoken with him a few times since last Sunday, but was getting annoyed with Andrew because he was so paranoid about getting caught for the robbery.

Tonight, Johnny had a late night party to attend at a fraternity house. It started out as a few guys getting together to watch a basketball game, but as the plans escalated, the event turned into an all-out party, filled with lots of alcohol and plenty of sorority girls. It sounded like fun. Right now he was just enjoying the peaceful stroll alone through the dark campus. There were a few lights placed along the sidewalk, but for the most part people stayed away from the interior of campus at night. He knew this party was going to be wild and loud, so for right now it felt great to walk through the quiet campus. The robbing and ransacking of Chesterton's home was the furthest thing from his mind. He tried to forget about it to avoid accidentally mentioning it to anyone and starting rumors around campus.

Approaching the large old frat house just after 9:00 p.m., he could hear the music blaring on the inside. A young looking freshman kid was already bent over in the bushes throwing up. Johnny ran his fingers through his long blond hair. He couldn't help but smile a bit at the sight of the freshman.

Walking up the old steps, he approached the door. The exterior of the house looked like a stereotypical frat house. The paint was chipping away on the exterior and the front door looked as if it was from the 70s. Johnny didn't bother to knock but decided to just head inside. Opening the door, the smell of beer hit him strongly, and he already noticed a large number of empty cans on the ground. The house was packed. He could see roughly seventy college students spread out among the living room, dining room, and steps. Some of them were dancing wildly in the spacious living room, while others just stood on the edge chatting.

"Welcome, Johnny man!" a large black football player welcomed him, giving him a hand shake and embrace, "Go grab a beer before we run out."

"Thanks, I will," Johnny said, walking away. He remembered meeting the football player, but he couldn't remember his name. Passing into the kitchen, he spotted many college kids sprawled over the tables and counters drinking and chatting. He was greeted by a few more students before he was able to grab a beer out of the refrigerator. He told himself he really needed to pace himself at this party as many intoxicated students were not going to be able to leave tonight.

Stepping back into the living room he ran into Dax, "About time you showed up. Where have you been, man?"

"I was just taking my time. I knew this one is not getting over anytime soon."

"I know what you mean, bro, I'm not even planning on going to class tomorrow. I'm in it for the long haul tonight!" Dax said, clearly bursting with excitement.

Johnny smiled, knowing that Dax was looking to stir up something crazy. He looked around for Angela, "Dax, have you seen Angela? She was going to meet me here tonight."

"Yeah, I saw her around here. That skinny kid who lives down the hall from us was trying to flirt with her."

"What an idiot!" Johnny said, shaking his head. Everyone on campus knew that messing with Johnny's girl meant trouble.

"Well, he's over there," Dax said, pointing to the far side of the room, "you can speak with him in person if you'd like."

Johnny could see the kid in a corner on the other side of the living room past all the kids dancing. He was a very skinny third or fourth year student who was always dressed in a buttoned-up collared shirt.

Dax continued, "He looks like he's trying to hide from you. I'd say let's go over there right now and set him straight." Johnny concurred, thinking that he could make a fool of this kid right away at this party. It was too tempting of an opportunity for Johnny to pass up. He passed through the crowd on the way to the far side of the room.

The kid saw Johnny coming his direction and he knew what was happening. He quickly turned to his left and looked for an escape. Seeing a door, he quickly turned the knob and opened the door frantically. Johnny and Dax were making their way through the crowd but were still about fifteen feet away. The kid entered the room and shut the door tight behind him.

Standing at the doorway, Johnny and Dax could see underneath the door that a light was on. Dax tried to turn the knob but found it was locked. "Step aside," said Johnny calmly. It was a very old door and it would be no problem for Johnny to pick the lock with a simple credit card.

It was a matter of just a few seconds when they heard the lock click. "Piece of cake," Johnny said under his breath. They opened the door quickly to find that the room was a bathroom. It was tiled beautifully with a classic black and white pattern. They could see the skinny college kid sitting curled up in a ball in the bathtub. His eyes grew wide as he saw Johnny and Dax enter the room.

If Johnny wasn't intimidating enough, Dax's towering height would surely frighten anyone. "I guess it's never a bad time for a bath," Johnny said sarcastically.

The kid spoke up in terror, "Listen, I'm sorry, I didn't do anything. I was just at the…"

"Shut up, boy!" Dax shouted, interrupting him mid-sentence, "What's your name?"

"Stuart, and look I was hoping I could explain what…"

"Why don't you cool off first," Johnny said, turning on the shower full blast, completely soaking Stuart. He tried to get out of the tub, but Dax quickly grabbed him by the face and threw him into the path of the water.

Johnny continued, "Let this be a simple lesson to you, Stu, not to mess with my girl." Dax then proceeded to grab a can of shaving cream from the counter and began spraying it on the poor college kid. Stuart began to cry a little.

"Please, just let me explain. I didn't do it," Stuart said, moaning as he spoke.

"Listen, kid, I think you've explained enough," Johnny said, feeling confident that justice had been served.

"No really, I don't know why she freaked out all of a sudden," Stuart said through his tears.

Johnny and Dax looked at each other puzzled. "What are you talking about?" Johnny questioned.

"We were just talking about life around school, and yeah I was trying to get a date, but I wasn't getting anywhere, and then all of a sudden she freaked out on me."

Johnny turned off the water. He was completely confused at this point, "Listen kid, tell me what happened and tell me now!"

Stuart wiped some of the shaving cream off his face. He was speaking frantically, "I don't know, man, like I said we were just talking, then all of a sudden she freaked, saying someone was after her."

"What?!" Johnny shouted.

"Yeah, she said he was here and coming after her."

"Who's here?" Johnny said, looking straight at Stuart, "Who is she talking about?"

"I don't know," Stuart said, shaking his head. "That's all I know, she ran off before I could get anything else out of her."

"Where'd she go?" Johnny demanded.

"Like I said, I don't know. She ran off. I couldn't see where she went."

Johnny grabbed Stuart's face, right around his chin, pushing his head into the wall. "Listen, you coward, you tell me the truth, and you give it to me now," he said looking squarely into Stuart's eyes.

"That's it! That's it. I promise that's all I know. I promise. I promise," Stuart said, breaking down into a full fledged cry. Johnny let go of his chin and he fell straight onto the tub's floor.

Turning toward Dax, Johnny continued, "We've got to find her."

"Yeah, but who would be after her, especially knowing she's your girl?"

"I don't know, man, but whoever it is, is going to pay," Johnny said, getting angrier by the second. "Look, you check outside and see if you can find anything. I'll check with some of the guys around the house and see if anyone saw where she went."

"Gotcha," Dax said, walking out of the bathroom. Johnny followed behind, entering the large living room. The college kids were still drinking and partying like it was the end of the semester. Johnny found no interest in it at the moment. He scanned the crowd, looking for Angela. It was hard to get a good look at everyone with drunken college kids running around like fools. Johnny made his way through the crowd, lightly pushing some of the kids out of his way.

He wondered where she could be. He checked the kitchen and dining room area. Many of the kids in those areas were calmly chatting. It appeared to be the place to go if one wanted to stay out of the ruckus of the dance floor. Johnny scanned the faces of the kids. No sign of Angela.

Leaving the kitchen, Johnny checked a few of the downstairs bedrooms. Most of the rooms he found well kept and unattended, save for a passed out college kid lying on the floor in one of the rooms. Johnny wondered if Angela could have left without him seeing her. He mainly hoped that whoever had spooked her was gone by now.

He entered the living room again to find Dax descending the main staircase, "Dax, did you see anything? Was she up there?"

"No, no sign of her, but I did run into a couple guys that thought they saw her leave."

Johnny still had many questions revolving in his mind, "Huh, I wonder when she left."

"The guys said it wasn't long ago, maybe fifteen or twenty minutes at the most."

"What? That can't be right," Johnny was puzzled, 'That would have been right before I arrived. I would have seen her on the way out. That can't be right."

Dax was calm, "Look, man, that's just what the guys said. They said they saw her leave."

"They saw her leave? What door did she go out of?"

"They said through the side door that leads to the garage. It is by the dining room area, and…"

Johnny left before Dax was finished. Things were not adding up and he was extremely puzzled. He quickly passed through the kitchen and dining room and headed for the side door. Dax was following close behind. Reaching for the door, Johnny turned the handle.

Catching up with Johnny, Dax put his hand on the door, just above Johnny's head, preventing him from opening it. "Johnny, calm down, man, why's this so urgent? She probably just left and went home."

Johnny looked squarely at Dax. He looked a little frightened, "She didn't go home. She would've left just before I arrived. The garage door wasn't open when I came, and I would've seen it closing if it was just before I arrived. Something's just not adding up, Dax." Dax let go of the top of the door. Now he understood where Johnny was coming from.

Johnny slowly opened the door and went inside. It was a single car garage that was very old and dusty. He flipped on a light switch as they entered. The light was dim and barely helped. In fact, it gave the garage a very eerie feeling. It looked as if the garage was used to store a lot of miscellaneous junk for the fraternity guys. Johnny saw an old bed frame, along with some broken patio furniture, a lot of rusty car parts on some shelves, a dilapidated bench-press and weights, and boxes upon boxes scattered around on the floor.

Stepping down the entry steps, Johnny wondered what he was looking for. There didn't seem to be any other way out of the garage besides the main door for cars. He stepped further into the middle of all the junk and looked around briefly. He thought he heard a mouse scurry by. Just out of curiously he decided to look into one of the boxes. Opening it up, he found a bunch of dusty glassware. He chuckled to himself, shutting the top of the box.

Taking a deep breath, he figured Angela probably left through the front door, and he somehow just missed her, "Well Dax, I guess the guys were wrong. I don't think she left through the garage after..."

Johnny jumped back in horror. Someone had grabbed his arm. He knew it wasn't Dax since he was still standing at the doorway. Catching his breath, he turned around and looked through a stack of boxes by the wall where he was standing. There he spotted her. Angela was sitting against the wall curled up in a ball. Johnny could tell by the way the makeup was running down her face that she had been crying. She was clearly shaking with fear.

"Angela!" Johnny shouted.

"Please, please, Johnny, don't let him get me," she pleaded, shaking her head. Dax came over to join them.

Johnny crouched down close to comfort her. "Angela, what are you talking about? Who's trying to get you?"

"He's here, Johnny, he's here!"

"Who's here?"

She continued as if not even hearing Johnny, "He's been stalking me subtly all week, terrorizing me. At first I thought it was just some stupid prank by someone at EIU, but his notes have gotten more specific and more threatening as the week's gone on."

"Angela, you've got to listen to me. Who's stalking you? Who's coming after you?"

"Chesterton!" Angela said, pleading.

"What, he's here?"

"Yes, Johnny, I saw him, and he's coming for me. He sent me a note from across the room, telling me not to leave. I don't know what to do."

Johnny looked right at Angela, trying to calm her, "Look, we are going to get you out of here and then take care of this jerk later."

She grabbed a hold of Johnny's arms, "Listen Johnny, he knows. He knows what you guys did to his house."

Johnny looked up at Dax, who was shaking his head in anger. Dax decided to chime in, "If it's a fight this old man wants, then we'll give it to him. I'm not going to be punked down by nobody."

Angela continued, "Johnny, please don't mess with Chesterton. Just give back what you took from him, and try to make all of this go away."

Johnny was curious, "What does he want?"

"I'm not sure," Angela spoke between tears, "Something you took. Something that is vital to his tricks."

Chapter 10

——⟋⟍⊙⟋⊙⟋⊙⟋⊙⟋——

FRANKIE WAS LOOKING FORWARD TO a quiet evening with his family. Frankie's family always had dinner together on Thursday nights. Though attending the fraternity party with Johnny and Dax was tempting, Frankie wouldn't miss a family dinner for anything. His family lived in a quiet community about a half hour northwest of the college. His mother's Italian cuisine was a favorite item of gossip in the quiet community.

Frankie couldn't help but smile as he pulled into the driveway of the small ranch house. His family had moved from the New York City area about eight years ago. His father had accepted a very lucrative position from a John Deere plant in Iowa and it required relocation. His two older brothers followed suit, both finding terrific jobs at the plant. Frankie's older sister also worked in the area as a university professor at the University of Northern Iowa. Though they all greatly missed New York, they were all thrilled to be in Iowa together.

Frankie entered the house to find his oldest brother, Paolo, setting the table. He was still dressed in his professional work clothes. He looked like a very well-to-do business man. "Frankie, how ya doing, bro?" he said smiling.

"Hey, I'm doing fine, big bro. How 'bout with you?"

"I could only be better if Maria and the kids were joining us tonight. There's a bad flu being passed among the kids, and she thought it best to stay home with them."

"Sorry to hear that, I hope they get to feeling better soon," Frankie said sympathetically.

"Frankie! Welcome home, Son!" his dad said, entering the dining room along with his mom, sister, second oldest brother, and his wife.

"How's my baby boy?" his mother said, reaching out to give him a big hug.

"I'm fine, Ma, thanks for having me," he said, squeezing her tight. Frankie loved his family dearly. He appreciated how loving and supportive they were of him, despite the fact that he was not as talented, nor as intelligent as his older siblings. In many regards he felt like he was the black sheep of the family. He struggled in school; his grades were subpar, and he always rode the bench when he actually made it onto an athletic team. So far in life he had fallen far short of his siblings. He was always looking for some way to perform on their level, either academically or athletically.

While at Eastern Iowa University, Frankie wondered if he had finally caught his break when he met and befriended Johnny Platt. The past couple of years had catapulted Frankie's popularity around campus. He didn't even care that he was known as one of Johnny's lackeys; he was just thankful that people were noticing him and remembered his name. It was everything he had ever wanted.

"Well, we're just about ready to eat," his dad announced. "Frankie, why don't you put your books away in the back room and then help your brother set the table."

"Sure thing, Pop," Frankie said, forgetting that he had carried his backpack in with him. He retreated back to his old bedroom to put his books down. He was thankful that his parents had kept his room intact. Frankie quickly threw his backpack on his old bed and turned to head back into the dining room.

About to step out of his room, he stopped and turned, looking at his backpack on the bed. He thought he saw something odd when he threw it onto the bed. He stepped back toward his bed and reached for his backpack, turning it on its side. He saw one of his side pockets was slightly open with an envelope sticking out of the side. Pulling it out of the side pocket, he stood staring at his name written on the front.

He turned it over and tore the seal on the back. Reaching in the envelope he pulled out a small card about the size of an index card. There was one sentence written in the middle of the card in cursive. It read:

What would you do to protect the ones you love? - Chesterton

Frankie immediately dropped the card onto his bed. He wondered if this was some bad joke from Dax. He hadn't thought of Chesterton the last couple days. He had felt guilty for breaking into Chesterton's home and had tried his best to forget all about the incident. This note brought everything back into his mind in an instant and he felt ashamed. He would be content if he never heard the name Charles Chesterton again.

He took a seat on the end of his bed and picked up the card. He did not recognize the handwriting and knew for sure it was not Johnny's. *Who would do this? Could this really be*

Chesterton? He asked himself. He wondered what was meant by the question.

Johnny tried to open the garage door, but found it was jammed. He was trying to find some way to quickly get Angela out of there. He could tell she was legitimately terrified. He was worried about her. Even though Johnny often lost his temper with her, he truly did care for her and wanted to get her to safety.

"Let's just bring her back through the house," Dax said. "There's a back door on the other side of the kitchen."

Johnny walked back over to where Angela was sitting and tried to help her onto her feet. "C'mon, baby girl, we're going to get you out of here," he tried to reassure her.

"I can't Johnny, I just can't," she spoke through her tears. "Please don't make me go through that house again. I don't want to see him. Please Johnny!"

"Shhh, it's going to be all right. It's a short walk through the kitchen to the back door. If anyone tries to mess with you, Dax and I are going to knock 'em out. It'll be all right, people don't mess with Johnny Platt."

Angela slowly got to her feet. Dax walked over and draped his lightweight coat over her shoulders, even putting his hood over her head. She appreciated it, not wanting anyone to see her crying eyes. Johnny grabbed her elbow and slowly led her to the door leading back into the house. He peeked inside to make sure everything was clear. He felt as though Chesterton was watching his every move.

"All right, come on, Angela," Johnny said pulling her through the doorway. Most of the partiers ignored them, which Johnny was thankful for. He wanted to get out of this house as soon as possible.

Reaching the door, a young looking freshman kid came up to Johnny with a beer in his hand and started chatting a mile a minute. "Johnny Platt, how you doing, man? I live one floor below you. I came over to see if you wanted to hang out and talk some…" The kid was not able to finish because with one swift punch Dax hit him right on the nose, knocking him off his feet and into a kitchen counter. Johnny didn't have any time to deal with a situation like this and Dax knew it. They quickly forgot about the kid as they exited the house.

Getting Angela out the door, she collapsed onto the grass and started crying heavily again. Johnny bent down to comfort her. "Angela, believe me, Chesterton's going to pay for this. I don't care what it takes or costs. He's going to regret the day he ever messed with you."

"Johnny, please, just leave him alone. I don't want you getting yourself hurt, and I think he is…"

Dax couldn't help himself. He was getting madder by the moment. "Oh, you talk about someone getting hurt. Chesterton's gonna have a whole new definition of pain when we get finished with him. Ain't that right, Johnny?"

Johnny slowly rose to his feet, "He'll regret the day he ever messed with Johnny Platt."

"Frankie, you about ready? Dinner just came out of the oven," his dad yelled from the other room.

"Sure… I'll be right there," he said, still deep in thought. The small note made him afraid. He wondered if his parents would somehow find out about the incident. They had raised him better than this. He quickly hid the note under his backpack and headed for the dining room.

The table was arranged as beautifully as ever with an extravagant candle center piece. Paolo had already set all the plates, utensils, and napkins in their proper places. "Thanks for your help, little bro," he said sarcastically. "What took you so long?"

"Oh, I was just looking over some, uh… papers I got back from earlier in the day. Yeah, just looking over some stuff."

Frankie's mom entered the room carrying a large dish of pasta. "All right, everyone, sit down before the food gets cold." Like obedient children they all headed toward the table. Family meals were always important and everyone knew to come to the table immediately when called. Frankie's mother never had to ask twice.

As everyone was finding their seats the doorbell rang. "Oh my," said Frankie's mom, "Just when we all sit down, one of those door salesmen always comes by." She quickly got up from her seat and went to the door.

"How are your studies going, Frankie?" his sister Rita asked.

"They're going well, trying to stay afloat here before finals week. I think they're going to be brutal this semester."

"Well, don't forget to get plenty of sleep at night," his dad spoke in his thick Italian accent. "You know I don't like it when you hang out with that blond headed boy late at night. It's not good for your health, son."

"Oh, come on Dad, lay off of the poor boy," his brother added. "He's got to have a little fun. He's in college after all."

"Well it's just not good for a boy with his studies to be out so late. The boy needs his rest," his dad spoke passionately with his hands. "And where is Maria? The food is getting cold."

Frankie couldn't help but smile at the care his family showed toward him. He appreciated how they looked out for him and took an interest in his life. They were the anchor in his life of hard times and trials. It was through his family that he learned to be polite and treat others with kindness. They taught him the value of a dollar and how to work hard. He loved them dearly and did not know what he would do without them.

After a few minutes Frankie's mother returned to the table. "Sorry about that, you will never guess who that was."

"Who was it?" his dad questioned.

"It was that nice man at the farmers' market that sold me the spice for this pasta tonight. He was just so nice, and he said he lived not too far from here. I told him where we lived, and he just stopped by, being neighborly."

"Well, Maria, why didn't you invite him in? Didn't you think I would want to meet our neighbors?" Frankie's dad said, slightly frustrated.

"I told him we were just sitting down for dinner and he didn't want to disturb us."

"Ok, well I'm hungry, let's pray," Frankie's dad concluded. Everyone bowed their heads and closed their eyes. Frankie didn't hear a word that was said during the prayer. His mind went right back to the note in his backpack. More specifically it went back to the question expressed on the card. He would do anything for his family. It didn't matter the cost or the extent. He loved them, and that was all that mattered. He wondered what was really meant by the question.

"Amen," his dad said loud and clear. Instantly everyone started passing dishes and putting dressing on their salads. The meal seemed a little odd with Frankie's nieces and nephews missing, but it was nice having a quieter meal for a change. Frankie helped himself to a large serving of pasta.

"Frankie, don't you be taking all the pasta. You be sure to leave some for the rest of us," his brother said. Frankie could only muster a smile as his mind was still on the note. He looked up at his brother, but out of the corner of his eye saw his sister. She had a strange look on her face. It looked as if something disturbed her or rather she was eating something strange.

"This pasta has a very odd taste," his sister said. "I can't place it, but it seems like it has a fruity taste to it."

"Yeah, you're right," Paolo added, "it's like a faint pineapple taste. Ma, aren't you strongly allergic to…"

"Maria!" Frankie's dad shouted.

It all happened so fast and Frankie only caught a glimpse of her falling from her seat. Everyone quickly got up from their seats and ran over to her. She was coughing and making loud heaving sounds. She was curled up in a fetal position. "I'll call 911," Paolo shouted, quickly taking out his cell phone.

"Maria! Maria," his dad pleaded, "Breathe, breathe, my love! Oh God, please may she be all right." He sat down beside his wife, cradling her head in his lap. He could hear his brother in the living room giving directions to a dispatcher.

Frankie felt paralyzed with horror. He wondered who came to the door before dinner.

Chapter 11

─wwoଚ୧৳ଚ৳ଚ৳ଚ৯o৵w─

ANDREW DECIDED TO GO BACK to his classes on Friday. His arm had healed rather quickly and didn't seem to be much of a problem. He was still living with fear and anxiety, wondering if anyone would find out that he had broken into Chesterton's home. He also imagined that his grades had tanked since he had missed a lot of assignments and didn't bother to complete them while he was at home. He had always been a straight A student, so he anticipated the disappointment in possibly failing a couple of classes.

His parents had been gone most of the week, attending to Elliot in the hospital. His condition was worsening as time progressed. Doctors had noticed his nose swelling to an unhealthy proportion, and the infection was getting worse. He was also maintaining a fever of around 102 degrees. His parents took the week off of work to attend to him. Andrew was pleased with the silence around the house this past week. He didn't want anyone asking him more questions or encouraging him to get out of the house. He had wanted to be alone and to wait a few days before returning to school.

Currently, walking through the hallway of the general education building, Andrew found himself paranoid, constantly looking over his shoulder. He wondered if it was a good idea to return to school today. The message he received in the hospital greatly frightened him. He also wondered if it truly was Chesterton dressed as a doctor, or if, in his paranoia, he was imagining things. When he had awakened from his concussion there was a different doctor attending to him. Whether it was Chesterton or not, it still frightened him. He kept thinking about Sophia's warning about Chesterton. His magic show was wonderful and impressive and Andrew wondered what this magician was truly capable of.

Andrew had about five minutes before class. He saw Johnny in the hallway approaching him. "Drew, what's up man? You look awful," Johnny said. He could tell Andrew looked worried.

"Yeah, it's my first day back and I'm just trying to get back in the swing of things. I think I missed a lot of assignments."

"Look, man, I don't know what you're doing tomorrow night, but Dax and I are headed back over to the casino tomorrow. We're going to pay another visit to our little friend Chesterton."

"What?" Andrew responded, "Are you sure that's a good idea?"

"Listen, Drew," Johnny said, running his fingers through his shaggy blond hair. "This guy paid a little visit to Angela last night at the party. I think he's been stalking her all week."

Andrew couldn't believe what he was hearing. He kept nervously readjusting his glasses. He wished he could just get away from all of this. He was speechless, trying to quickly think of something to say to change Johnny's plans.

Johnny continued, "It looks like Chesterton is an old fashioned kind of guy. He wants to handle things man-to-man, and so that's exactly how we're going to settle it with him."

"Johnny, I think we should just leave him alone. Hopefully everything will settle down and Chesterton will let it go and…"

"Look, Drew, no one messes around with Johnny Platt and gets away with it. He will regret the day he ever met me," Johnny sounded cool and confident, but also a little angry at Andrew's comment. It was only slightly reassuring to Andrew. He continued, "Andrew, let's meet up at my place tonight and we can come up with a plan."

Once again Andrew felt as if he was standing on the edge of a cliff, wondering what he should do. He wanted out of everything, but knew he was in far too deep to simply walk away. In the back of his mind he knew Chesterton was watching him. He also knew that Johnny was depending on him, and no one simply walked away from Johnny Platt. Andrew responded the only way he felt he could, "Ok, I'll be over to your place tonight, about 7:00."

It was impossible for Andrew to focus on the physics lecture. He didn't take any notes or even look up at the professor much. His mind was preoccupied with Chesterton and the robbery. He sat with his notebook in front of him and pencil in hand. Occasionally he would doodle or write something arbitrarily. He was trying anything to relax. Periodically he looked over at Johnny who was as cool and calm as ever. Johnny was trying to take notes, and he even looked like he was paying attention to the lecture. Andrew was jealous, wishing he could look as passive as Johnny.

All of this left Andrew in a quandary. He felt as if he both loved and hated Johnny. He loved him for his confidence and his poise. In many ways he wished he could be Johnny Platt. But the other half of him hated Johnny. Andrew hated him for bringing him into this situation with Chesterton. He hated him for the constant paranoia of the past week. He hated him because he felt trapped, unable to walk away from this mess he had created. It was like he was in a cage, and for that he wished he'd never met Johnny Platt.

The clock showed 10:30 a.m., and class was dismissed. Andrew quickly packed up his notebook and threw his backpack on his back. He had another class in ten minutes, though he really felt like skipping it and going home.

Johnny caught him by the shoulder, "Drew, remember my place tonight. I'll see you around 7:00."

"You got it, I'll see you there," Andrew said, giving him a slight nod. Andrew noticed the dean of students standing at the doorway of the classroom. At first sight Andrew was a little terrified, thinking that the dean was coming for him. Instead, he appeared to have his eyes fixed on Johnny. Andrew decided to make a quick exit before he was dragged into another mess.

When most of the students had left, the dean made his way over to where Johnny was standing. He was a tall man, roughly 6'4. He wore glasses and was dressed in an old fashioned brown suit. He couldn't have been more than 45, but he always seemed to dress many years older than his age.

"Johnny Platt, may I have a word with you?" he said in a deep, hollow voice.

"Dean Keller, how are you, man," Johnny said, condescendingly. He knew he had gotten the best of the administration in the past, and he wasn't afraid to show his confidence around them.

"I've had better days, Johnny. Can you follow me to my office?" he responded, pointing his hand toward the classroom door.

"All right, but let's keep this quick, Dean, I got things to do. Lots of homework you know," Johnny returned, mockingly.

Upon arriving at the dean's office, Dean Keller sat professionally behind his desk and Johnny took a seat on one of the guest chairs. Keller decided to get right down to business, "Johnny, we've had some problems with our databases here at the school and…"

"Listen Dean," Johnny interrupted, holding up his hand, "I haven't been messing with your databases. I think you got the wrong fellow." Johnny was halfway telling the truth. In the past he had manipulated the school's records and databases, but it had been at least a year since he had done anything like that.

The dean continued, "No, Johnny, the problems we were having were miniscule. We had them fixed, but in the process of everything we found a number of red flags that showed up in your records."

"Like what?"

"Yes, there are numerous unpaid student fees, some even going back to your freshman year."

"What?" Johnny said stunned.

"Our records also show that you've failed to pay your room and board the last couple of years, along with a large portion of your tuition."

The dean was correct. About a year ago Johnny had hacked into the school's software system and hid this debt from the administration's records. He stood up in anger, "You can't pin this on me now, Dean. The semester is just about over. You can't be saying that all of a sudden all this new debt has magically appeared."

Dean Keller was still calm, "Johnny, it's not like you have a whole bunch of new debt. Rather, this debt was always there, it just wasn't showing up. Normally student debt, especially of this magnitude, would have numerous red flags attached to it. Those flags weren't there before but have now shown up when we reset the software."

Johnny couldn't believe it. Dean Keller was right. All the debt that he was talking about was legitimate. They both knew it. The dean had known for the last couple of years that Johnny was manipulating the system; he just didn't have any proof. Dean Keller continued with a smile, "Here, I can print off a list of the debt you owe, and I want to remind you that there is no way for you to proceed with your education or graduate until you deal with this debt."

Johnny stood there in the dean's office stunned, waiting for the paper to print out. He wondered how this had ever happened. He had been flawless in covering up his pranks and mischief. He thought they would never find this hidden debt. There was no way he could go back and erase everything. These records were probably copied and made extra secure this time. He knew the administration would never let him get away with this twice.

Johnny truly wondered how he had gotten caught. A thought came to mind. He spoke up, "Dean, one question for you."

"Oh yeah, what's that?" he said, taking off his glasses.

"What was the name of the name of the company that fixed the school's software?"

Dean Keller was taken aback, "I'm not sure, our computer department outsourced it to a small business in town."

Johnny breathed heavily in frustration, "Do you remember anything about it? Is there anything you could tell me?"

Dean Keller shrugged his shoulders, "I don't know, I just remember some guy named Charles working in the office a couple days ago."

"Charles?" Johnny said, astonished.

"Yeah, that's right, real friendly guy."

Later that night the three guys, Johnny, Andrew, and Dax, along with Angela met up in Johnny's dorm room. Johnny was fuming, similar to the weekend before when he had been humiliated during Chesterton's show. Now, he was ranting about his student fees and couldn't believe Chesterton was crafty enough to manipulate the university's software. Dax sat quietly on the couch, sipping a beer, and a part of him seemed amused by the challenge Chesterton had presented. Angela was a different story. She sat against the window on the floor, clearly scared. Chesterton had frightened her deeply. She was wearing a large Eastern Iowa t-shirt along with sweatpants. Her hair was pulled back in a simple ponytail and she wasn't wearing makeup. Though she was still beautiful, Andrew thought she looked much different without her makeup. The fear in her eyes terrified Andrew.

Johnny continued pacing the floor of his living area, "If Chesterton wants a fight, then a fight we're going to give him. I'm going to hit this character where it hurts. He's going to pay for all of this and pay big. Drew, do you still have those blueprints of the tricks you took from him?"

Andrew had forgotten all about the tricks he had stolen from Chesterton. He was trying hard to forget about the night they broke into his house. "Well yeah, I've got them, do you want them?"

"Of course I want them," Johnny shot back, pulling on his hair. "We are going to learn the secret of his stupid tricks and outsmart him at his own game if you know what I'm sayin'."

"What are you talking about, man?" Dax said, taking a sip of his beer.

"We sabotage his show, revealing his tricks to the audience as he does them. We'll ruin him and show everyone who this clown really is."

Dax shook his head, sitting up straight in his chair, "That'll never work, man. You know Chesterton's got that place flooded with security. We're not going to be able to say or do anything with them watching us. They will see us coming a mile away."

Johnny picked up a nearby textbook and threw it in frustration. He knew Dax was right. Chesterton probably knew they were going to retaliate and would probably warn all his staff about the boys coming back. They would be watched like hawks. Dax kept going, "Johnny, you may just have to walk away from this one. Count your losses and go home. I mean we did trash his house, man, maybe he thinks we're even now. Let's just let it go."

Angela started tearing up just slightly. Andrew wasn't sure if it was from the intensity in the room or the idea of letting Chesterton go. Either way, he could tell that somehow Chesterton had hurt Angela deeply. She seemed terrified of Chesterton in a much deeper way than any of the guys were.

Noticing her tears, Johnny walked over to her, sat down beside her and put his arm around her. She gently leaned her head against his chest. Johnny let out a deep breath. He spoke quietly and with more control, "I don't think he's finished yet. He's still toying with Angela, sending her messages and randomly calling her. Dax, we have to stay ahead of him."

All of this was news to Andrew. He knew Chesterton had been stalking her, but he didn't know to this extent. Andrew thought it all made sense. The most direct way to a man's heart is to attack the beauty that he loves. Especially to Johnny, Angela seemed like his trophy around campus. All the guys knew she was off limits, and no one would dare to mess with her unless they were willing to bear the wrath of Johnny Platt.

Everyone in the room sat silently, contemplating the mess they were in. Andrew hoped that somehow Dax's suggestion would win out. He didn't want to mess with Chesterton anymore and hoped that this was the end of it. He never wanted to think of Charles Chesterton again, much less see him again.

They were all deep in thought when they heard a knock at the door. "Who in the world is that?" Johnny said, a little confused. All of them were fearing the worst, knowing that Chesterton had been disrupting their lives and showing up around campus. Dax quickly got up from his chair and grabbed a small red baseball bat Johnny had in his closet. Dax was always up for a fight and his tall 6'5 height was intimidating to just about everyone. He approached the door, gripping the bat tightly in his right hand. He reached out with his left and slowly opened the door.

A thousand scenarios played through Andrew's mind. He wondered what would happen if Chesterton was on the other side; he feared Chesterton would go to great lengths to make them pay for the break-in. He also feared the police. What if Chesterton simply turned them in? His blood could probably be found in multiple spots in the house. He was guilty and there was no way out of it. Once again he felt as if his life was on the edge of a cliff.

To the relief of everyone in the room, it was only Frankie. He quickly pushed the door further open and came inside. They could all tell he was extremely angry. Andrew thought he looked like a bull, ready to charge at any moment. He took off his hat and threw it to the ground in anger.

"Frankie, what's up, man?" Johnny said, puzzled.

"He's after us, Johnny. He knows we did it," Frankie returned, his New York accent seemed stronger than ever.

Dax spoke up, "You're way behind the times, Frankie. We're debating whether to keep messing with him, or if all this is over and we should just walk away."

"Oh, you better believe this isn't over. He messed with my family. Family is important to me, and no one messes with them and simply walks away."

Dax shook his head again, "Frankie, we already talked about all this. We got to leave this guy alone. He knows we would probably go after his house again, or even disrupt his show. He'd be waiting for us, man."

Frankie was pacing angrily at this point, "Oh no, we are going to settle this like men. I'm going to teach this guy a lesson he never learned."

Johnny spoke up, "What are you thinking, man? I got to admit Dax is right. We can't try anything during his show."

"Oh no, I'm not talking about his stupid show, I'm saying we wait for him at the end of the night and literally bash his face in, straight gangster style. I've already checked with a couple friends I have working at the casino. I know he leaves quietly every night through the back door by the dumpsters. We wait late, catch him off guard, and jump him."

All eyes looked toward Johnny, still sitting beside Angela. He was calm, thinking about Frankie's proposal. Andrew hoped all of this would be rejected immediately as foolish. Johnny rose to his feet and looked squarely at Frankie. He ran his fingers through his long shaggy hair, "Fine, if Chesterton wants a fight, we'll literally bring him a fight. Tomorrow night we'll settle this thing."

Chapter 12

—⟿⟾⟿⟾⟿—

IT WAS EARLY ON SATURDAY morning, not long past 7:00 a.m. Andrew hadn't slept much that night. His mind was fixated on Chesterton. For the past week he had thought about him constantly. He wondered if he would ever be free of this situation. His new fear was that the plan of confronting him after his magic show tonight would not help things but might only make them worse.

Andrew sat on his bed looking at the two items he had stolen from Chesterton's home: the ring and the card. The ring was old and worn and looked as if it was something from Chesterton's previous life: his life before performing magic. He tried to read the writing on the sides, but it was too well worn to make anything out, except maybe a letter here or there. Andrew slipped it on his finger and found it a near perfect fit. Holding his hand up to the window, he tried to see if the outside light would give him any hint of what was written on it. He still couldn't shake the feeling that he had seen it before. He wished he could remember where. Everything was so unclear to him.

He heard a knock on his door. He quickly took the ring off and put it under his covers. "Come in," Andrew said hesitantly. His dad, Jerry, opened the door and stuck his head in. He didn't look good. His beard looked unkempt and there was sadness in his eyes.

"Hello, son," his dad said quietly, "Your mom and I are going to head up to the hospital. There's some unusual swelling in Elliot's nose and the doctor is concerned about it. They're going to run some tests on him and make sure his infection isn't getting any worse."

"Oh...ok," Andrew returned, "Well, let's hope for the best."

"I was going to ask you if you wanted to go with us. You haven't seen him since you got your stitches. Elliot would probably like to see you."

"Thanks Dad, yeah, umm... I better not today," Andrew said, trying to think of an excuse. "I just went back to school yesterday and I'm trying to get things in order, so I better not today. Hopefully, if he's still in there tomorrow, I'll stop over and see him."

His father looked clearly disappointed. "All right, son, well... you rest up." He backed up and started closing the door, but then he stopped and opened the door again. He looked puzzled as if something had caught his eye. He turned his head slightly to the side to get a better angle on what he saw. "Andrew, what's that?" He said, pointing toward the bed.

Andrew looked down at his bed spread to see Chesterton's card sitting in plain view. The backside of the card was up. The silver plating looked beautiful shining off his bedroom light. There was no way for Andrew to lie and say it was an ordinary playing card or just something he had found. It was too striking to pass it off as ordinary. "Oh, this thing," he said, holding it up. He searched for words, "It's just something one of the guys at school gave me. He was cleaning up some old stuff and passed it off to me."

His dad was taken aback. He could usually tell when his son was lying and Andrew thought it was probably obvious this time. His father had a very inquisitive look on his face. He stood staring at the card for a few seconds, but it seemed like an eternity for Andrew. He wondered what his father was thinking.

"Well, Dad, I need to get started with my day, so if you will excuse me, I'm going to go ahead and get dressed," Andrew said, trying to snap his father out of his trance.

"Oh yeah, right, right," his dad returned. "I'll see you later, son. Give us a call if you need anything or want to check up on Elliot."

"Sounds good, Dad, I'll call you later." Jerry backed out of the room, shutting the door tight. Andrew was glad his father didn't ask any more questions. He was in fact a little relieved.

Looking at the card, Andrew wondered if Chesterton missed it or knew it was gone. Even though Chesterton was an extraordinary magician, most of his tricks revolved around common items, such as cards, rings, etc. Andrew remembered the cards falling out of Chesterton's sleeve at the end of the performance. To the best of his recollection, this one looked like one of those cards.

Flipping it over, he saw the single heart in the center of the card with an A in two of the corners. From this side, it looked no different than a normal playing card, a simple Ace of Hearts. Andrew wondered if this was the only Ace of Hearts in the deck or if it was from a trick deck with many duplicates of the same card. If that was the case, maybe Chesterton didn't notice that one card was missing.

Andrew's cell phone rang. Reaching for it on his dresser, he saw that the call was from Johnny. His heart sank at seeing Johnny's name. He wished so much that Johnny might have left him alone that morning. He so badly wanted a few hours of peace before the show tonight. He answered, "Hello."

"Drew, sorry it's early, but we need to go ahead and get started. If we are going to physically take down Chesterton, then we need to make sure we have all our bases covered. I want to be sure Chesterton doesn't know what hit him."

"Ok, what do you want me to do?" Andrew said, wiping the sleep from his eyes.

"Meet me at my place in a couple hours. Me and Frankie are heading down to the casino to plan things out a little more thoroughly. Things are slow over there early on Saturday morning, so hopefully security will be a little more lax."

"Right, I'll be there," Andrew said, trying to sound confident.

"Cool, see ya."

Hanging up the phone, Andrew threw it across the room. He pulled on his hair in frustration. The reality of the situation was starting to get to him. He couldn't imagine assaulting a man, or even being an accomplice to such a plan. He wanted to be free, but didn't know how. "God, help me," he prayed in frustration.

Dax spent a lot of his time on Saturdays working and this Saturday was no exception. *Big Bob's Beef Burgers* was a local fast food chain. It was popular among Iowans, and more specifically college students. They were known for unique hamburgers, which consisted of loose ground beef as opposed to a patty. Dax didn't particularly like the job, but the pay was decent for a fast food restaurant.

This particular Saturday Dax was working the register, decked out in his navy blue apron and his white paper hat. He didn't like dealing with the people, but he appreciated not having to work with the greasy hamburger meat today. At the moment an elderly lady was trying to figure out what she wanted to order.

"Now, Sonny, what exactly is a beef burger and why does it come with curly's fries?" the elderly lady asked, trying to comprehend the menu.

"A beef burger is the same thing as a hamburger, but the meat is loose," Dax responded, annoyed.

"Well, does it fall out everywhere?" she asked, worried.

"No, it's not too bad, maybe a little, but you'll be all right."

"But I don't want it spoiling my outfit. Can't you just make me a hamburger, son?"

"No, I can't. This is *Bob's Beef Burgers*, we don't make normal hamburgers here. You can either order a beef burger or get out of here," he said looking directly at her and annunciating clearly. The woman must have been about 90, and she was very confused, but Dax didn't care. He was just looking for any way he could to get rid of this lady.

The woman looked very sad. "But I don't know where to go. My son dropped me off here while he went to the hardware store. He told me to eat something before he comes back."

Dax was completely tired of this situation and didn't care the least bit about helping her. He saw one of his teenage coworkers wiping off some tables in the back of the restaurant, and thought of a quick plan. "Listen, lady, you see that boy wiping off tables in the back there?"

"Yes?"

"Why don't you go ask him all your questions? He's really good at answering questions from old ladies. I'm sure he'll be a big help to you."

"Oh, thank you so much, Sonny. You are one nice, tall fellow."

"Sure, don't mention it. Now, go talk to him," he said, waving his hand forward in an effort to shoo her away.

With that, the lady left him and headed toward the back of the restaurant. Dax was relieved she was gone. He quickly took off his hat and laid it on the counter. No one was in line and he glanced out the door and didn't see anyone coming. He looked in his back pocket and pulled out an old pack of cigarettes. He didn't smoke much, but whenever he got a little stressed he craved one.

He walked to the back of the kitchen where his team was working feverishly because of a backed up drive through. "Hey, could someone cover for me?" Dax asked, "I'm going to take a quick smoke break while the line is clear."

His shift manager, who was browning the meat, took a quick look toward the front of the store. He then looked at Dax, "Looks like a guy just came in. If the line is clear after him, then take a break."

Dax cursed under his breath. He turned around and headed back toward the front counter. He stuffed the cigarettes back into his pocket. Arriving at the counter, he reached for his hat and quickly put it back on, adjusting it slightly. "May I help..."

He was unable to finish; the sight of the man in front of the counter stopped him mid-sentence. They stood staring at each other for a few seconds. "Nice to see you again," he responded.

Even though he was dressed in jeans and a grey polo, Dax knew exactly who he was, Charles Chesterton. He was clean shaven this time and his hair was nicely parted, like someone from the 50s. He smiled slightly.

"What do you want?" Dax said, staring.

"Well, this is *Big Bob's Beef Burgers*, so I guess I'll have a burger and fries," he said in a sarcastic tone.

"No, I mean, what do you really want?"

The grin on Chesterton's face got big and looked more sinister. He shook his head ever so slightly. He appeared to be enjoying the moment. "Well, if in case you have forgotten, it was you and your friends who disrupted *my* show, and then broke into *my* house. I guess the proper question would be, 'What do you want with me?'"

"How do you know it was us?"

"Oh, come on," Chesterton seemed a bit irritated at the question, "Don't play games with me. You may have disabled my security system, but the whole house gave it away. You boys need to cover your tracks better."

Dax didn't know what to say. He felt as if he was at the mercy of Chesterton while he was at work. "Why don't you just get out of here and leave me alone?"

Chesterton smiled again and looked to be deep in thought. Dax could tell he had some diabolical plan brewing in his mind. Chesterton leaned over the counter placing one hand down beside the register, and with the other he motioned for Dax to come in closer. He looked around to see if anyone was watching, and with a quiet voice he whispered, "I've been wondering the same. Why don't you leave me alone... Lanky."

Dax's eyes got big and his mouth dropped open. A flood of memories came to his mind. Memories he did not want to go back to. He looked straight into Chesterton's eyes and became frightened. He wondered who this man truly was at heart.

Dax and Chesterton stood looking at each other silently for a few seconds. There wasn't a single movement in Chesterton's face, when all of a sudden, in one quick move Chesterton blew a puff of air into Dax's eyes. Dax was taken aback and took a couple steps backwards. He was surprised, completely taken off guard for a moment. He found himself beginning to blink his eyes rapidly. They began to water. He started to wipe them, but the more he wiped them, the more they watered, and the more they watered, the more they began to burn. Dax screamed out in pain and dropped to one knee. He held his eyes tightly, trying fiercely to get them clean. He yelled out in panic, "Help me, help me."

A few coworkers stopped what they were doing and went to attend to him. They were confused, asking him what had happened and if he needed an ambulance or to be driven to the hospital. The manager noticed Dax was clutching his eyes, "Let's take him to the bathroom and try to rinse out his eyes." Three of the workers picked him up and tried to direct him to the staff bathroom in the back of the kitchen. The restaurant became a place of panic. The few customers that were in the restaurant wondered what was happening. Many of them got out of their seats and walked toward the counter to get a better look. None of the workers were at their stations anymore; they were all trying to see what they could do to help.

They reached the bathroom door and were about to push it open when Dax stopped them, "Wait, wait, wait…" He said, putting his hands out, trying to stop the commotion. "I think I'm good," he said, breathing heavily. The pain had suddenly subsided and had left just as quickly as it had come on. He wiped his eyes one last time and began to open them slowly. The world looked a little fuzzy, but quickly became clear.

His coworkers looked shocked, looking at his face. Dax wondered what they were thinking. He was trying to think of an explanation when he noticed that his coworkers were looking at his face in horror. He quickly put his hands back up to his face and felt the bumpy irritated skin around his eyes. One of the teenage employees was the first to speak up, "Dax, you… don't look so good, man."

Dax pushed open the bathroom door and looked at himself in the mirror. His eyes were clearly red with irritation, but he also noticed that the skin around his eyes had broken out, looking like severe acne. He did not look normal. It was like he was wearing a pair of acne goggles around his eyes. His skin felt so tender.

At that moment his mind raced back to his conversation with Chesterton. He quickly left the bathroom, pushing his coworkers out of the way, and weaving through the kitchen, back to the front counter. Most of the customers had gone back to their seats and things seemed to be fairly back to normal. Dax noticed that Chesterton was gone. He peeked out the side door, but saw no sign of him.

Dax stood at the counter thinking about his conversation with Chesterton. He was gripped by both fear and anger. He did not want Chesterton to get the best of him. He thought about the guys' plan tonight, and he felt even more of a drive to make it happen. Dax wanted to give him a taste of his own medicine.

Dax was deep in thought when the elderly lady came back to the counter, "Can I still have some of those curly's fries, Sonny?"

Chapter 13

ANDREW SAT WATCHING KIDS GO up the climbing wall. This section of the Waterloo Casino was packed with families this afternoon. He was hoping he would be lost in the large crowd and would not be noticed by anyone. It was about fifteen minutes before Chesterton's show would begin. The doors were already open and people were starting to enter the auditorium.

He kept going over the plan in his mind. Johnny, Dax, and Frankie were hiding out back behind the casino, close to where Chesterton's car was parked. They were hiding among some old boxes near a couple dumpsters. Chesterton usually left the casino about an hour and a half after his show ended, and through his inside connections, Johnny learned that Chesterton always left through the back kitchen door, close to the dumpsters. He figured this was the best way to avoid any media or small town paparazzi. The boys' plan was to ambush Chesterton, jump him, and basically just rough him up.

Andrew fiddled with the ball cap he was wearing, along with his fake mustache. Johnny wanted him in disguise. Andrew's part was to be the lookout man. Via text he would let Johnny know when Chesterton's show ended, as well as keep a look out in the parking lot when the attack occurred. They figured Chesterton wouldn't go to the police since he didn't with the break-in, but Johnny still wanted Andrew to keep a look out for them just in case someone spotted the attack and called the police. He was very thankful for this job; he didn't want to take part in the actual assault. He knew if they were caught he would still be seen as an accomplice, but for the moment he felt relieved that he didn't have to beat anyone up.

The line for Chesterton's show was starting to get long, and Andrew thought this was a good opportunity to sneak in without being noticed. Getting in the back of the long line, he reached for the ticket in his pocket. His hand was a little sweaty. Thankfully Johnny had set him up with a seat in the high balcony, about as far back as one could get in the auditorium. They didn't want any chance of Chesterton recognizing him in the crowd.

The line moved more quickly than Andrew had expected and he was already at the ticket collector. "Ticket please," he said routinely. Andrew held his out without saying a word. The man quickly tore it and gave it back. "Upstairs, take the first stairwell on your left," he said, not missing a beat.

Before entering the auditorium, Andrew took one more look at the kids ascending the climbing wall. He was envious of them. More than anything, he wished he could be one of those kids. They were simply laughing and enjoying themselves with their families. He longed to be away from all this anxiety he was feeling. He longed for peace. Andrew simply wanted to be with his family. Hanging his head, he entered the auditorium.

He went up two flights of stairs and eventually found his seat on the next to last row of seats in his section. The auditorium was dimly lit in this region and made for finding one's seat a little difficult. The dark of the auditorium gave Andrew a greater sense of reassurance that he would not be seen by Chesterton. He quickly sat down and pulled out his phone. He wrote a quick text to Johnny, "Found my seat, show set to begin in 7 minutes."

It was just a few seconds later that Johnny wrote back, "THX, let me know when he comes on stage."

The last few minutes before the show began seemed to take hours in Andrew's mind. He sat nervously in his chair fiddling with his mustache, which was starting to come off from the sweat on his face. He could feel his heart beating rapidly in his chest. It was hard to believe that it was just one week ago that he was sitting in this same auditorium with Sophia right beside him.

The lights began to dim, and people began to clap. Andrew looked up to see the curtain rising and Chesterton walking under it. He was dressed the same, in his tuxedo and top hat. He was clean shaven this time. He smiled politely to the crowd, mumbling the words "thank you" under his breath. The crowd began to quiet when he took off his top hat and held it in his hands. He greeted the crowd, "Good evening ladies and gentlemen. Thank you for coming to my show."

He then began his speech, "Every magician has a repertoire of tricks that he regularly performs. These are his favorites…"

Andrew reached for his phone again to send Johnny a quick text, "Chesterton on stage & giving his intro." Andrew tried to hide the phone as he wrote the text. Cell phones were prohibited during Chesterton's performance.

He continued to hear Chesterton's voice in the background, "...A magician often becomes complacent and disinterested in his own tricks. He must look for..." Chesterton spoke very eloquently, annunciating every word, clearly for the audience to hear. Andrew thought he had a wonderful voice.

Johnny quickly wrote back, "THX, let me know when it's over." Andrew promptly put his phone back in his pocket. He hoped to not have to get it back out until the show was over.

Chesterton's show once again was marvelous. Andrew would have very much enjoyed it under different circumstances. He started, once again, with Chinese linking rings and proceeded from there. The show ran pretty much the same as it had the last time Andrew had seen it. He pulled rabbits out of hats, levitated various objects he brought on stage, and pulled roses and other flowers out of volunteers' jackets and pants pockets. The tricks were great, and Andrew felt that, once again, Chesterton's execution was marvelous. He was mesmerizing to watch.

Strangely, Andrew found himself smiling during parts of the performance. Chesterton used humor as he dazzled the audience. He was very witty and always seemed to know the right thing to say at the right moment. Andrew's mind drifted to Sophia who was sitting beside him last time. He remembered how much she enjoyed the show, despite his lies. He wished she were beside him again, simply enjoying the show.

As the show was nearing a close, Andrew wondered how Chesterton was going to end it. He wanted to see what Chesterton had originally planned the last time. Chesterton spoke, "And now, ladies and gentlemen, I want to end the show a little differently tonight." A large cage was brought out, and it looked as if he had planned some type of grand escape while the cage suspended in mid-air. Andrew felt like he could he could hear the disappointment among the crowd.

The woman sitting beside Andrew leaned over to her husband and Andrew could hear her say, "Oh, I really wish he would do his multiplying card trick. That was my favorite last time." Without realizing it, Andrew's eyes got big. His mind went to the silver card he had taken from Chesterton's home. He knew it was probably used in the trick. Andrew became frightened, thinking about it. He wished it was not in his possession.

A young lady was helping to tie Chesterton up in chains and the trick was about to begin. Andrew felt his phone vibrate in his pocket. He thought it would be Johnny wondering how much time the show had left. Taking the phone out of his pocket, he realized it wasn't Johnny. Andrew didn't recognize the number. It wasn't a local number. Someone from a different area code had sent him a text. He slid open the phone and pushed the view button.

Andrew began to shake with fear as he read it, "I really wish I could have my card back. It's a favorite among my fans. –CC"

Andrew dropped the phone and began to breathe heavily. *Who sent me this text?* he wondered. Was this a cruel joke from one of his friends, or had Chesterton found him? He looked on to stage to see Chesterton glance his direction. He gave a small wink as he continued with his cage trick.

Andrew was terrified.

Johnny sat among a pile of cardboard boxes behind the casino. He could peek through just enough to see the back utility door of the casino. Frankie was hidden on the other side of the door among some trash bags and Dax was in a tall dumpster. Even though the area stunk, they knew it was what it took to ambush Chesterton.

The plan seemed too easy. When Chesterton came from the door, Frankie would quickly spring forward and slam the door shut. Johnny would grab Chesterton and pull him aside behind the dumpster where Dax was hiding. All three guys would then go to work on beating him up. Traditionally this would not have been Johnny's style, but Frankie insisted. He wanted revenge for the harm Chesterton had done to his mother. She was still in the hospital being treated for an allergic reaction along with poisoning. Frankie was not going to let it go. His anger was motivating him and making decisions for him. Reason and logic had long ago left his thinking.

Johnny could feel himself breathing heavily as he sat among the boxes. It was a hot April night and all three guys were sweating profusely. They were dressed in all black, similar to the night they had robbed Chesterton's home. They also had dark ski masks on, only exposing their eyes. Johnny worked hard at controlling his breathing while he waited patiently for Chesterton.

He was focused intently on the door when he felt his phone vibrate. Looking down at it, he saw a message from Andrew. Opening it up, he read it closely, trying to suppress the light, "Show over, but have a bad feeling. Something doesn't seem right."

Johnny wondered what this message meant. He wondered if Andrew was just being paranoid like he had been all week. Johnny thought maybe he was getting a little nervous about the whole plan. He considered aborting the mission, but he wanted more info from Andrew before he quickly called everything off.

He started to reply to Andrew's message when the back door began to slowly open and they saw Chesterton emerge from it. Johnny quickly put the phone back into his pocket. Something didn't feel right; this was much earlier than they had expected

Chesterton to leave the casino. Without having time to consider the circumstances, Johnny saw Frankie jump from the trash bags and spring toward the door. He slammed it quickly and pushed the man toward the boxes where Johnny was hiding.

Johnny threw the boxes aside and grabbed him. He was still dressed in his top hat and tuxedo, which was unusual for Chesterton leaving the casino. They took him behind the dumpster and without warning Frankie began pounding on his stomach like he was in a fierce boxing match. After a couple of Frankie's punches, he fell to the ground holding his stomach. Frankie did not let up; furiously he began kicking at his shoulder and torso.

Johnny stood amazed at Frankie's fury. He had never seen such anger in him. Johnny feared Frankie was not going to let up and might possibly kill him. Grabbing Frankie by the arm he spoke under his breath, "Frankie, let up, man. You're going kill him if you keep going like this."

He turned to face Johnny, speaking harshly, "Shut up, Johnny, this man was out to kill my mother. I'm going to make sure he never forgets this beating." Pulling his arm away from Johnny, he went on delivering angry kicks to the torso.

Frankie stopped for a moment, but he was still breathing heavily. Johnny could tell he was in deep thought. Looking over at Johnny, Frankie proceeded to pull off his ski mask. "What are you doing?!" Johnny shouted.

Frankie gritted his teeth as he looked at Johnny, "I want him to see the man who is beating him. I want him to fear me, like we are fearing him."

Frankie bent down and pulled the top hat off his head. He threw it aside. Bending down he grabbed a handful of brown hair, pulling his face off the ground. Frankie looked nearly possessed. His anger and fury consumed him. Johnny wondered where all this anger came from.

Looking into the man's eyes, Frankie came to a horrid realization… the man was not Chesterton. He stood up in shock and horror. Johnny froze wondering who this man was. He did greatly resemble Chesterton, but even in the dim lighting they could clearly see that this was not the magician.

Andrew quickly stood from his seat after he wrote the last text to Johnny. He was shaken by the supposed text message from Chesterton. He just wanted to go home. He didn't want to look out for anyone. He just wanted to escape and go somewhere far, far away.

He walked down the balcony steps in a hurry. He looked down to see that the top of his shirt was sweaty, like he had just finished exercising. He was nervous, not wanting to be noticed or seen by anyone. Passing through the auditorium doors, the sights and sounds of the casino overwhelmed him. Andrew felt light-headed, but knew he had to press on.

Trying to exit the casino, he bumped into a middle aged woman. "Excuse me!" she said, turning around to look at him.

"I'm sorry," he said, sounding out of breath.

"Are you ok, Son? You don't look so good," she said, shaking her head.

Andrew felt a greater rush of paranoia hit him as she said this. He felt like the world was watching him. He felt eyes everywhere, thinking in the back of his mind that everyone knew about his plan. "I'm fine, thanks," he said, waving his hand. He knew he had to make it out of the casino.

With a laser like focus he walked straight to the front doors of the casino. He tried to pass through the revolving door casually. He thought the doors were moving so slowly. Eventually, passing to the outside of the casino, he let out a deep breath. The outside air was hot.

He began to walk slowly toward his car. His silver Mustang seemed like it was parked miles from the front door. He wished he could have just run to it, but that would be too suspicious.

Andrew's breathing began to slow with each step. He felt more relaxed the closer he got to his car. He was going to make it, he kept telling himself. Reaching into his pocket, he grabbed his keys. Just a few more feet and he was going to be home free. His hand was shaking a little as he put his key in the door. Unlocking his door, he breathed deeply, trying so hard to relax.

Opening the door to his car, he heard something coming. Looking up, he realized it was a siren. He could see four Waterloo police cars coming up the road toward the casino. He quickly got into his car, thinking for a moment they might be coming for him. He soon realized that they sped past him toward the casino. He kept watching as they continued on toward the back of the casino, the same place Johnny, Frankie, and Dax had been hiding.

"Frankie, let's get out of here now!" Johnny said with urgency in his voice. "We don't know who this guy is."

Frankie swiftly bent down and pulled the man up, forcing him against the dumpster. "Who are you?" he shouted.

The man stood fearfully, looking into Frankie's eyes. He didn't say a word, just stood stunned.

"Answer me!" Frankie shouted.

The man shook as he spoke, "Listen, I don't know what's going on. I was told to come out the back door wearing this outfit. That's all I know... I swear."

"You're lying!" Frankie shouted back.

"No, no I promise you. I was just told to go through that door at about this time. I don't know anything."

Johnny didn't want any part in this. He looked around to see if anyone was watching, and then turned to Frankie. "Frankie, listen to me, man. Let him go, let's get out of here, now!"

Frankie paid no attention to Johnny as he stood face to face with the man. "Who sent you? Who sent you through that door?" Frankie said, nearly pressing his face up to the man.

"Please, don't hurt me. It was Chesterton. He told me to do it. I think he knew you'd be waiting for him outside these doors."

"Then why'd you do it? Didn't you know someone was just going to rough you up out here? Why'd you do it?" Frankie countered.

The man's eyes opened wide and he shook as he spoke, "Because I fear him. You don't know what he is capable of. You don't want to mess with Charles Chesterton."

That was all Johnny needed to hear. Looking around one more time, he quickly ran off into the woods that bordered the back of the casino for a few miles. If he had to, he would run seven miles to the next town. He knew they were in way over their heads this time. He ran as fast as he could.

Hearing Chesterton's name again seemed to infuriate Frankie even more. He began beating the man further, punching him continuously in the stomach. The man screamed in pain as Frankie delivered each blow. He tried to fall to the ground, but Frankie picked him back up and continued to deliver punch after punch.

He was totally focused on letting out his anger when the police pulled up. They could easily see Frankie beating up this helpless man. They quickly emerged from their cars and pounced on Frankie. They threw him to the ground and cuffed him in a matter of seconds.

Chesterton smiled as he watched from an upstairs window. It was quite a scene to behold.

Johnny had run for about a mile and a quarter straight when he decided to stop. He had come up on a stream in the woods. He collapsed by it and took off his mask. He splashed a little water on his face and on his hair. It felt cool. Leaning against a tree by the water, Johnny decided to take a break. He figured he had run far enough to escape any pursuit that may be coming his way.

His mind quickly went to Frankie. When Johnny was just a few yards into the woods he could see the blue lights coming toward them. Johnny knew Frankie had been caught. How he wished Frankie had just run away with him into the woods. He thought Frankie was probably looking at a couple of years in prison. Johnny wondered if his name would be brought up in any discussions with lawyers or during a trial. It worried him, but more importantly he wondered what his next move would be, or better yet, he wondered what Chesterton's next move would be.

Fatigue started to settle in. Johnny shut his eyes as he started to fall asleep. It was a peaceful setting with the sound of water in the background. He was about to completely doze off when a thought came to his mind. It awakened him. He was puzzled. He wondered, *What happened to Dax? Where was he?*

Chapter 14

———————

Dax was packing his clothes into a large duffle bag. It was just past 1:00 a.m. He had his TV tuned to the local Channel 7. The news was unfolding about the attack at the casino. Frankie's name and picture were all over the news. He occasionally glanced at it as he continued to cram clothes into the duffle bag. He was only mildly interested in the news about Frankie. His mind kept going back to Chesterton. He was terrified at the thought of him.

In fact, Dax was so terrified by Chesterton that earlier tonight he had never even climbed into the dumpster. As soon as Johnny and Frankie got into their positions among the boxes and trash, Dax decided to quietly sneak away. Chesterton had uncovered a world of hurt with simply one word. Dax kept going over it again and again in his mind. He hated the very sound of the word… Lanky.

Dax had decided he was leaving Iowa once and for all. There were too many bad memories here. He didn't want to think of them any longer. He didn't care that he was at the end of a semester. If Chesterton was able to uncover a world of hurt with just one word, he feared what would later come. His mind kept going from fear to anger back to fear as he packed his bag.

The breaking news had run its course and it was on to infomercials. Dax quickly turned off the TV and threw the remote at it furiously. He hated life right now and didn't care about anyone. He was going to run away and forget all about Eastern Iowa and more importantly forget about Chesterton.

The thoughts kept running through his mind non-stop. He felt as if his head was going to explode. He sat down on a nearby chair, putting his hands on his forehead. Dax closed his eyes as he felt the tears begin to flow from them. He thought back to how it all started, approximately 12 years ago.

Dax was sitting in the principal's office, crying his eyes out. He hated how the other kids always made fun of him. He was by far the tallest kid in the 5th grade, and also, by far, the skinniest. He was quite a spectacle to look at, measuring just under six feet, with almost no meat on his bones. People would often point him out wherever he went. He also endured constant ridicule by other kids in his grade.

Today was exceptionally bad. Another kid had tripped him on the playground and Dax fell face first in a large mud puddle. A number of kids saw it and laughed at him. No one bothered to help. This eventually landed him in the principal's office when he refused to leave the playground and go back to class. What made matters worse was that the principal seemed annoyed with all his crying. Principal Jefferson sat behind his desk with his arms crossed, like he was in a business meeting, not with a crying elementary school kid.

"Listen, son," Jefferson said, "this is nothing to cry about. You just got a little mud on your face and it sends you in here crying like a baby." Of course this didn't help matters, and it only plunged Dax deeper into misery.

The principal continued, "I've called your father, and he's going to come by and pick you up since you refuse to go back to class." Dax's father was a hard man and would not take too well to him crying like this. Dax knew that this was all going to come back to haunt him.

It was just a few minutes later that Dax's father walked into the office. He was dressed in his work clothes and his hands looked quite dirty. He was a very tall man, measuring around 6'4, close to the height Dax would later reach in life. He sounded disappointed as he entered the office, "Well, I hear I have a son who ain't goin' back to class 'cause he got a little dirty."

The principal shook his head in agreement, "You're exactly right, sir. He refuses to go anywhere."

Dax spoke through his tears, "Dad, I'm sorry. I just didn't want see those kids again."

His dad shook his head, "Son, do you think this was worth me missing work for? I can't just skip out on my job whenever you don't want to face your problems. What's the matter with you?"

"Dad, I just couldn't take it anymore. I don't want to be here. They're just so mean to me, Dad."

His dad just rolled his eyes as he spoke, "Well that's life, Son. You can't just run from them your whole life. I don't care what they do to you."

Dax grew angrier by the moment. He took his hands away from his face and looked up at his dad. He shouted, "They don't even treat me like a person. They don't even know my name. They call me Lanky, they shout it at me, and make fun of me. All the time, they call me Lanky, Lanky, Lanky!"

Dax's father was surprisingly calm. His son's shouting didn't even seem to faze him. His father looked to be in deep thought when he answered his son, "Well, Dax, they call you that because… it's true. That's what you are, son. You are lanky." Principal Jefferson nodded his head in agreement. Dax erupted in a flood of tears.

The memory was painful. It made him angry, thinking about it. The only thing that brought him joy was the knowledge that Principal Jefferson was fired later that year. But then he thought about his father. Dax seemed to be a perpetual disappointment to him. The name Lanky became the nickname Dax's father would call him whenever he was disappointed with his son. Dax hated the sound of it, and he had hoped that by leaving home and going to Eastern Iowa that he would never hear that name again. It had stuck with him through grade school and even at home. He had hoped that it was gone forever.

Dax quickly finished packing. He was leaving many personal items in his dorm room. He didn't care what happened to them. He wasn't passing half his classes, so he didn't care about his education either. He just wanted to get away. Anger, sorrow, and especially fear had always followed him. This time, once and for all, he was going to run away from them. He threw his duffle bag over his shoulder and slammed the door as he left.

Frankie paced back and forth in his jail cell. The police station had a couple of cells in which they could keep a few low level offenders for a night. There wasn't much in them: a couple bunks, a sink, and a toilet. Occasionally an officer would come by and ask him some questions. He easily complied with the police; his anger was not for them.

Chesterton consumed him. The fact that Chesterton had outsmarted him and was probably resting comfortably in his house enraged Frankie like nothing else in this world. No one messed with Frankie's family and got away with it. He loved them dearly and felt they were the only ones who accepted him. He would do whatever it took to protect them.

Tonight he was sharing the cell with an old man who seemed to have gotten arrested in order to have a place to sleep for the night. He was starting to get annoyed with Frankie, "Hey boy, can't you settle down over there? I'm tryin' to get some sleep if you know what I'm sayin'." Frankie turned to the man and gritted his teeth. For a moment he thought about verbally fighting back, but then thought otherwise. He wasn't worth it. Looking back out the bars, he decided that calming down might be a good option. He sat down against the wall, as far as possible from the old man sleeping.

The reality had not yet sunk in that he was possibly facing jail time for assault. This would have large-scale ramifications toward his education and life in general. He thought about this briefly, and then shrugged it off. He felt his life was going nowhere. School was difficult for him and he never thought his degree or job skills were that impressive anyway. Frankie knew he could never measure up to the successes of his siblings. He always felt he would be the black sheep of the family. The least he could do was protect them.

After a moment, he thought about how lost his life had truly become. He had befriended Johnny purely in an attempt to make a name for himself, and for the last couple of years he was thankful for the popularity and recognition he had gotten. But it had all come to this night. He wanted to show both Johnny, as well as his family, that he could do something meaningful for them, something they would be proud of. He regretted being so anxious to confront Chesterton.

Frankie heard someone enter through the front doors of the police station. He wondered if he was going to have another cellmate for the night. He could hear the officers talking with the visitor. He could hear the conversation slightly and knew that visitor's voice sounded familiar. He quickly stood to see if he could get a glimpse of who it was. Frankie gasped in horror as he recognized the voice. A flood of emotions entered, and he became fearful.

Frankie started to cry as he saw the visitor being led back to his jail cell. He didn't know what he was going say. He was terrified of disappointing his brother. The officer escorted Paolo right to where Frankie was standing. His brother's eyes began to water as well.

"Hello, Frankie," he said very solemnly. Frankie burst out into full fledged crying; weeping heavily. The gravity of the night hit him like a ton of bricks.

Johnny spent most of the night in the woods. He tried numerous times to contact Dax, but it was in vain. Dax never responded. After running a few more miles from the casino, he eventually made his way to the highway. From there he was able to hitch a ride with a trucker back to the university. Johnny was thankful the trucker didn't ask many questions and kept to himself.

It was just before 6:00 a.m. when he walked into his dorm room. He found Angela sleeping soundly on his couch. The last couple of nights she'd been sleeping on his couch, not wanting to be in her room alone at night. Johnny was fine with it, knowing that the encounter with Chesterton had deeply frightened her. She was curled up in a blanket resting soundly when Johnny woke her up.

"Angela, wake up," he said, shaking her.

She slowly opened her eyes. She was startled to see Johnny still in his black outfit. She quickly sat up, "Johnny, are you just now getting back?" He didn't respond but walked over to his TV and picked up the remote.

"What happened?" Angela asked, still confused.

"I'll tell you what happened," Johnny said, sitting beside her on the couch. "Chesterton saw us coming. He planted a decoy that Frankie ended up attacking."

"What?"

"You heard me! Chesterton was a step ahead of me. He knew what we were planning." Johnny turned on the TV to the local channel 7. He wanted to see if the attack was on the early morning news.

Angela continued, "Where are the other guys? What happened to them?"

Johnny shook his head in anger, not making eye contact with Angela. He ran his fingers through his shaggy blond hair as he spoke, "Andrew was watching out for us and I figure he got away. Frankie got busted by the cops, who showed up right after I left. Thankfully, I made it to the woods and was able to escape all the chaos."

The morning news came on, and the opening story was the attack at the casino. Frankie's picture was shown on the screen, along with details of the attack. The news also reported that the magician, Charles Chesterton, had witnessed everything from his office window and called the police. According to the report Chesterton was unavailable for questions and did not want to speak to the media. Reporters then began to interview a number of witnesses who saw the arrest.

Angela seemed horrified at seeing Frankie's picture, and she even began to cry a little. Johnny stood up in anger. He tried to stay calm, but in a fit of anger threw his remote down against his coffee table, breaking the remote into pieces.

He was pacing around the room when he heard something in the report that caught his attention. The morning anchor said that as far as investigators were concerned, Frankie acted alone.

Angela couldn't believe it, "Johnny, did you hear that? The cops think Frankie acted alone. You should be ok! You don't have to worry about…"

"Shut up, Angela!" Johnny reacted harshly, "Can't you see what he's doing? Chesterton's messing with us. This is a game to him. He must have seen it all from his window, but yet he is letting me go. He doesn't want to turn me in because he wants to keep this going."

Angela didn't back down, "Johnny! Let him have this one. Just walk away."

"I can't walk away!" he shot back, "he's not going to leave me alone. It's like he wants something from me. Maybe something we took last week."

"Then give it back, Johnny, and walk away. This guy's too powerful. You don't mess with him. You can't beat him," Angela pleaded.

Johnny slowly turned to face her. Rage was building up inside of him. Angela struck a chord with him. He walked over the couch and got right into her face. He held his index finger in front of her eyes. She scowled as he spoke, "Don't YOU ever say anything like that again. I'm Johnny Platt, and no one messes with me in this town and gets away with it."

Angela began to cry harder. She spoke softly, "Johnny, please don't do this. I don't want him to hurt you."

Johnny eased up a bit, backing away, "Oh, don't worry about me. I know how to protect myself."

"What do you mean?" Angela said, confused. Johnny left the living area for just a few seconds and went to his bedroom. He came back with an old shoebox he had stored under his bed. Placing it on the coffee table, he slowly opened the lid. It was filled with old baseball cards from the late 90s. She continued, "Johnny, how is this going to help anything? What are you doing?"

Johnny was calm, "Sometimes you have to look closely to find what you are looking for." He pulled out a handful of cards and reached toward the bottom of the box. Angela couldn't believe what she saw as he pulled it out.

It was a pistol, relatively new, but it looked as if it had been used a little. Johnny admired it as he held it in the air. He smiled slightly, "Angela, in regards to protection, sometimes the best defense is the best offense. Instead of just sitting here and waiting for him, I'm going to head back to his house and finish this."

Angela stood up, shouting, "Johnny, are you crazy? You can't do this!"

He smiled as he looked straight at her and spoke calmly, "Watch me."

Chapter 15

ANDREW SAT ON THE FLOOR in his room. His back was against his bed. His shirt was off and he was thinking deeply about the current state of his life. He held Chesterton's silver plated playing card in his hand as he thought. He hadn't slept all night and was wondering what was going to happen to him. He wondered if Frankie would ever confess that he had accomplices. Andrew wondered if probation, jail time, or community service was in his future. He marveled at how his life had changed in a week's time.

Andrew was thankful that this past week Chesterton had chosen not to retaliate against him as severely as he had with Johnny or Frankie, but that didn't calm him. He knew Chesterton would soon strike him in a major way that he was unprepared for. He lived in fear of it this whole past week. He hadn't slept well and felt awful. He also thought about all the days of school he'd missed and knew his grades were suffering from the week of missed assignments. There was no comfort for him. This had been the worst week of his life.

Standing up he walked over to his mirror. Looking at his appearance, Andrew was caught off guard by how miserable he looked. In fact, he would say he hated his appearance. He had let himself go along with neglecting his hygiene this past week. He looked as awful as he felt.

Andrew heard a knock at the door. "Come in," he said, trying to sound casual.

His dad opened the door and entered his room, "Good morning, Son."

"Hey, Dad," Andrew answered. Jerry was dressed casually in a t-shirt and jeans. His hair was combed and his beard was trimmed. It was just before 8:00 a.m. and Andrew wondered where he was going so early in the morning. His first fear was that the police called and were coming for him. Andrew began to shake momentarily as this thought passed through his mind.

"Are you ok?" his dad asked.

"Sure, I'm fine," Andrew answered quickly, trying hard not to sound suspicious.

"Ok, well, Son, I'd really like it if you'd come with me to the hospital this morning. I know it's Sunday, but your brother's condition hasn't improved and we think it would really mean a lot to him if you were there."

Andrew was struck with fear and felt immobilized. He didn't know if this would be a good idea or not. The very fear of leaving his room seemed to be a mountain to climb. He didn't want to face the world. "Dad, I don't know if this is a good time. I just got a lot of things to do, and I was hoping to…"

Jerry put his hand up to stop him. "Andrew," he spoke very articulately, "This time, I'm not asking. I'd really like for you to come with me to the hospital. Your brother hasn't seen you all week, and your mother and I think it's best if you come down to see him."

Andrew sat for a moment trying to think of a defense. He went back and forth in his mind all in a matter of a few seconds. He didn't want to step outside his room, but yet the idea of being home alone in his own house frightened him as well. He felt paralyzed.

His dad continued, "Ok, go ahead and get ready. We'll leave in fifteen minutes." He then nodded politely and stepped out of Andrew's room, closing the door. The decision was made. He was going with his dad.

Andrew and his dad sat in silence in his dad's old pickup truck. Andrew sat staring out the passenger side window feeling paranoid every time they stopped at a light. He wanted to hurry and get to the hospital without seeing anyone or being seen. He felt as if he was going to faint when a cop passed them on the road. He had to keep telling himself, *everything's going to be ok. He can't watch you every moment. He's only one man.*

He wondered where his friends were and what they were doing. He had only received a quick text from Johnny saying that Frankie had been caught. Andrew wondered if this meant that he and Dax got away clean, or were chased away by cops. Even though it was killing his curiosity, Andrew hadn't texted Johnny back. He feared that Johnny was still going to get caught by the police and Andrew didn't want Johnny's phone receiving a call from him when the police arrested him. Andrew hoped and prayed that somehow his name would be cleared.

His heart sank when they had to stop for a long passing train. From the looks of it, Andrew knew they weren't going anywhere anytime soon. His luck seemed to be getting worse by the minute. Even though no one was around he purposely sank down in his seat a little. Every movement or sound brought on a new round of fear.

His dad let out a deep breath as he put the car in park. Andrew glanced at his dad as he began to speak, "Son, I wanted to talk to you about something." Jerry did not face his son but rather focused on the train. He didn't seem mad but very serious. Andrew could tell his dad had something heavy on his heart.

"What is it, Dad?" Andrew said, wondering if somehow he had found out about the incident the night before in the casino. He was afraid, but strangely a small part of him hoped his dad had found out. Andrew longed for freedom from this nightmare, hoping that somehow his dad could help.

"Andrew, I want to show you something," he said, pulling something out of his pocket. Andrew looked closely to see what his dad showed him. He couldn't believe it. He almost gasped. It was a ring, an old gold ring, similar to the one Andrew found in Chesterton's home.

Andrew didn't know what to say. He slowly looked up at his father's face and found his father staring back at him. He wondered what was going through his father's mind. He continued, "Son, I hope you will forgive me, but I went into your room yesterday evening after you left. The silver card I saw earlier in the day looked really suspicious. I knew you hadn't found it or come by it on your own. So I went in to get a closer look at it. Well, I couldn't remember where I'd seen this card, but I was certain I had seen it before. While examining it, I found the ring you hid from me, and I wanted you to know that I have one just like it."

Andrew's eyes got wide. He didn't know what his father was implying or what was meant by all of this. He was speechless.

A flood of questions was going through his mind. He was so shocked he didn't know what to ask or where to begin.

Jerry took the ring and put it back in his pocket. He continued, "Andrew, I've been watching Charles since he came back to town. I even went and saw one of his shows when he started performing. He was a friend of mine, not a close friend, but still a friend." He rubbed his beard as he spoke, "The ring you have is our old high school ring. We were in the same class and ran in the same circles. There was a group of us that caused mischief and were always looking for a new prank to pull. As a group, we all chose the same design of rings. It kind of became the symbol of our brotherhood."

The final car of the train was passing them and the cross arm was lifting. Jerry put the car back into drive and slowly drove over the tracks. "After high school we all seemed to mature and moved on. Many of the guys straightened up and just got on with their lives. Charles seemed to have the hardest time moving on. He didn't want to let things go. Eventually he moved on and took solace in magic or performing illusions. He became quite successful at it as I imagine you have seen."

Andrew swallowed hard, readjusting his glasses. He felt himself begin to sweat. He stuttered as he talked, "I…I…I'm sorry Dad. I know I'm not supposed to go to the casino, but I can promise you that I didn't gamble and play…"

"Shh…" his dad said, trying to calm him. "Listen, Son, that is the least of my worries. Somehow, and frankly I don't care to know, you have come upon some of these items from Charles and this brings me great concern. You do not want to be fooling around with this man. If he gave these to you at one of his shows then you need to somehow return these items to someone at the casino and then walk away. Do you hear me?"

"Yes sir," Andrew said, not knowing what else to do or say. He had so many questions on his mind. He couldn't believe that his dad knew Chesterton and was an acquaintance of his.

Jerry spoke up as they approached the hospital, "One more thing, I'm not going to tell your mother about this, but Son, I have to say you really upset me this time. I raised you better than this. No more going out to the casino. I don't want you seeing any more of Chesterton's shows."

"Yes, Dad, I'm so sorry," Andrew said, on the verge of tears. He looked back out the passenger side window. He didn't want to face his father anymore. He knew he had disappointed him and disappointed him deeply. He also felt sorry for the things his father didn't know: the partying, the drinking, skipping school, the robbery. It had been a horrible week for him.

Pulling up to the hospital, they found a spot in the visitor section. The parking lot was very empty on this particular Sunday. It started to rain slightly. Jerry put the car into park, and started to reach for the door handle. Andrew spoke up, "Dad."

"Yes, Son."

He had one question he wanted to ask before they got out, "Have you spoken to Charles Chesterton since he's been back?"

His dad closed his eyes. Everything was quiet except for the rain on the windshield. He spoke quietly, "No Andrew. I haven't, nor do I want to. That man is like a caged bird and in his heart is something very dark."

Jerry slowly opened the door to Elliot's hospital room. Andrew was following close behind his father. The door opened smoothly as they entered the room. It was dark. Andrew immediately saw his brother lying on the hospital bed with a gown on. He was lying on his side in a fetal position. He looked as if he was resting comfortably. Andrew's mom, Diane, was next to him in a chair. Her gaze was fixed on her younger son until they walked into the room.

"Andrew!" she said, quickly rising from her seat and embracing him. She squeezed him tight and held on for at least thirty seconds. She pulled back, looking directly into his eyes, "Thank you for coming. He will be glad to see you when he wakes up."

Andrew just shook his head as he looked back at his mother. She then went over to where Jerry was standing and embraced him tightly. Andrew glanced at his parents and noticed that his mother was crying as she hugged her husband. He wondered if his brother's condition was getting worse and if the doctors had found the proper diagnosis.

He heard his mother whisper to his father, "They say the infection is spreading and may be working through his bloodstream. The doctors say they've never seen anything like this."

Jerry squeezed her tight with his big arms. He spoke softly, "Shh… we'll get through this one step at a time. We've gotten through many trials in this life. This is just one more mountain to climb. Don't worry about a thing. We're going to beat this."

Diane pulled away, wiping her eyes. Jerry's words seemed to be just the right thing she needed to hear at the moment. She turned her gaze back toward Andrew, "Why don't you go over and say hello. I saw him stirring a few minutes ago. He might wake up."

"Ok," Andrew said, not fully knowing what to say. He, of course, never came clean about breaking his brother's nose. In fact, he hadn't even thought of Elliot much this week with everything else that was happening.

"We'll give you two a few minutes alone," Jerry said, "I'm going to take your mother to get a quick cup of coffee."

"Sounds good, Dad," Andrew answered. They left the room, gently closing the door. Andrew walked over to the chair where his mom had been sitting. He didn't want to wake his brother, particularly because he was the only one who knew the truth of his broken nose.

Sitting down, he looked at Elliot's face. It looked awful. It was swollen with infection and was a deep red. His eyes looked the worst. Yellow pus was crusted around the edges, along with fresh pus seeping from them. Andrew had to turn away from looking at them.

He started to feel guilty knowing that he was the one who put Elliot in this position. He truly loved his brother and didn't like seeing him in this state. He hadn't asked much about his condition, but he truly wondered at the severity of it. With each passing thought, Andrew seemed to feel worse and more responsible. *How could I have done this to my brother? How could I have put him in this state?*

He was lost deep in thought, staring at the floor, when a thought crossed his mind. Andrew remembered what Frankie said about his family and what Chesterton did to them. He remembered how Frankie's mom had been attacked chemically. Could Chesterton have done the same thing with his family? Truly nothing seemed to be off limits with this man.

The more Andrew thought about it, the angrier he got. Surely Chesterton was behind this. It was a simple break in Elliot's nose; nothing should have caused this type of infection. This was Chesterton's fault. Andrew rose from his chair and began pacing the room. The fear he had from this morning seemed to instantly turn to anger. Andrew thought about coming clean and turning Chesterton in. He felt as if this would be easy to prove. Surely the police would search his home and find some type of drug or chemical used in infecting their families.

Andrew was boiling over with anger when he felt his phone buzz in his pocket. Pulling it out, he saw a text from Johnny, "Where r u?"

He quickly responded, "Allen Hospital with my bro."

It was just a few seconds later when Johnny replied, "Meet me n the parking lot n 10."

A few minutes passed before his mother and father entered the room again, each carrying a small cup of coffee in hand. His mom was the first to speak, "Is it ok if we come back in? Did you have enough time with him?"

"Yeah, he didn't wake up or stir much. He still seems like he's out of it, sleeping heavily."

All three took a seat around the bed. Andrew sat by his feet, while his parents sat close to his side. Andrew kept his eye on the clock, waiting for Johnny. His mother and father talked softly so as not to wake Elliot.

"Did the doctor say when they were going to give another round of antibiotics?" Andrew heard his father say.

Diane coughed slightly as she answered, "No, they only want to give him a couple doses a day. It's rather strong they say."

"Hmm... well hopefully we'll get another report soon," Jerry said, patiently.

"Yeah, the doctors have..." Diane said, pausing to cough, "they have been doing a good job at keeping me... (cough) ... informed. I hope it stays... (cough) (cough) (cough)."

"Darlin' you don't sound too good," Jerry said, patting his wife gently on her back.

"I'll be ok. Since last evening this cough has come on strong at certain times (cough) in the day. I'm not sure what it is."

"You may want to get that checked out," Jerry said with a little bit of concern in his voice.

"I'll be fine, really (cough). I'm sure it will pass before the day is over (cough)."

Every cough seemed to resonate in Andrew's mind. It was almost like he could hear Chesterton laughing in the background. He looked toward the floor, putting his hands over his head. The coughs became more frequent and seemed to get stronger as the minutes passed. With every cough his anger grew. Chesterton had gone too far this time. First his brother and now his mother. How could he do this do to him? Andrew clinched his teeth as the anger swelled.

"Are you all right, Son?" Jerry said, seeing that his son seemed to be staring at the floor.

"Yeah, I'm fine," he said, quickly collecting himself. "I think I just need some fresh air." Andrew quickly got up and left the room. He couldn't take any more of his mother's coughing, and he was growing paranoid at the thought of her passing out at any moment. He felt trapped; he had to leave.

He felt his phone vibrate. It was Johnny. "I'm here," the text read. Andrew quickly walked to the elevator and headed down to the lobby. He noticed the waiting room was filling up now that it was mid-morning. Passing through the front entrance and walking into the parking lot, he saw Johnny leaning up against his two-door Honda. He quickly hurried over to where he was standing. Johnny looked flustered and unkempt. His eyes were red and swollen like he hadn't slept and had been under stress. He was dressed in dark green Eastern Iowa sweats.

As he approached Johnny, Andrew looked around to make sure they were alone. "Johnny, what happened? Is everything ok?" Andrew said, trying to keep his voice down.

Johnny looked off into the distance as he began to speak. He seemed to be at the end of himself. "Drew, they got Frankie. I don't know if you've seen the news, but Frankie's picture is everywhere. They got him locked up downtown and will probably end up shipping him to County. He's looking at doing some time."

"What happened? Did you see Chesterton?"

"No," Johnny said, shaking his head. "Chesterton saw us coming. He sent a decoy out, and Frankie didn't notice and jumped before he thought. The cops then showed up and cornered Frankie, catching him in the act of assault."

Andrew paced slightly, taking in the news of Frankie's arrest. "What about you and Dax? Did you get away?"

"Dax, I haven't seen or heard from. It seems he bailed on us early on in the night. I checked his room and it looks like he left."

"What do you mean left?"

"I mean he left, Drew," Johnny said emphatically. "It appears he packed up some of his things and left, like left school, and is gone. I don't know where he went or anything."

"And what did you do?" Andrew said, craving for answers.

"I took off as soon as I saw the cops coming. I don't think anyone came after me. I hid in the woods and made my way up north for a few miles, eventually coming to Highway 218 and catching a ride with a trucker back to school."

So many questions ran through Andrew's mind. He didn't know where to begin, "Well, are they coming after us? Did Frankie talk about us?"

Johnny ran his fingers through his hair, "I don't know for sure, but all the reports state that Frankie acted alone, which is a good sign for us."

"What about Chesterton? Do you think he'll tell them? What's he going to do?"

Johnny shook his head as spoke, "Well, that's the thing, Drew. Chesterton claims he saw the whole thing and says Frankie acted alone. He knows we were involved."

"What do you mean?"

"It means he's toying with us, man," Johnny said, starting to get upset. "He knows what he's doing. He's just trying to mess with us. He doesn't want us arrested. He could have called the cops on us a long time ago if he wanted to. I think he wants to take us down one by one. He's not ready to end this."

"Johnny, what are we going to do? We can't sit around and just wait for him to strike us again. I can't live like this, man," Andrew said, pouring out his heart.

"Well, I'll tell you what we're going to do. We really are going to finish this. If he doesn't want to get the cops on us, then we're going to take this opportunity to strike."

Andrew could see the anger in Johnny's eyes. "What do you have in mind?"

"I mean this," Johnny said, holding down his arm and letting the barrel of his pistol slide down his arm, just past his sleeve. "We've got to get him before he gets us."

Seeing the pistol, Andrew took a step back. His eyes got big. He couldn't believe what Johnny was suggesting. As crazy as this week had been, he never imagined it would come to this. He spoke quietly, "You can't be serious, man! We can't do this!"

Johnny slid the pistol back up his sleeve. "Think about it, Drew. He's definitely going to come after us again and he's going to strike hard until he breaks us. We won't see it coming." Andrew looked off into the distance, hoping and praying that Johnny was wrong, but knew in his heart of hearts that he was right. Andrew closed his eyes and tried to contemplate what Johnny was implying.

Johnny continued, "Think about this, too. He's not going to stop with just us. He's going to go after your little church girlfriend, along with your family. No one's safe, man, until we take this guy out."

Andrew's mind went back to his brother lying in the hospital bed. Would Chesterton take his brother to the grave? And what about his mom? Was this the beginning of her being hit with some deadly disease? He couldn't bear the thought of it. His anger came back with a fury. Truly, he did want an end to this. He looked back at his friend. He saw the confidence in Johnny's eyes. Andrew knew Johnny had a plan, and he wanted to hear it, "All right, I'm listening. Tell me how we're going to get rid of Charles Chesterton."

Chapter 16

It was late Sunday evening. Andrew was once again in his room putting on his black shirt and pants. He could feel his hands tremble as he pulled the shirt over his head. He couldn't believe he was going to do this again. After last weekend's raid, he had vowed that that would be the last time he broke into someone's home.

Earlier in the day, Johnny had laid out a plan as to how they would strike Chesterton. They would both sneak into his home. Andrew would come in through a side kitchen door and Johnny would scale the outside of the house and come in through a window a few minutes later. Andrew would act as bait and attract Chesterton's attention as best as he could. Meanwhile, Johnny would wait for a perfect opportunity to ambush him while he was distracted by Andrew. The plan seemed so simple. In fact, in Andrew's mind it seemed a little too simple, but he didn't have a counter plan, and he didn't want to disobey Johnny, especially when he had a gun.

Andrew checked his flashlight. It seemed like a very dark night. It was currently about 10:30 p.m. and they were hoping to enter Chesterton's home around midnight. He could easily leave his house because his parents were planning on spending the night in the hospital with Elliot.

Andrew quickly threw on his green Eastern Iowa sweatshirt. He first had to head over to the university to pick up Johnny and he didn't want to look suspicious in his black shirt.

He was about to leave his room when he felt his phone vibrate. Looking down he saw a message. Strangely this time it was from Sophia. It read, "Did u see Chesterton in the news today?"

He first thought about ignoring the text, but instead simply responded, "Yes."

He waited just a moment, and then saw she quickly wrote back, "Crazy! I hope your friends weren't involved. Folks ought to leave that man alone."

Andrew chuckled a little at the irony of her text. If only he had listened to Sophia's wisdom in the first place, all of this might have been avoided. He wished he had never set foot in the casino that night. It was crazy how much life had changed since that day.

It was a minute later and his phone vibrated again, "Sorry to hear about your bro. I'll be praying for him."

He quickly wrote back, "thx."

Slipping his phone into his pocket, Andrew headed for the door. How he wished he could just sit in his room and text Sophia. He longed for a simple life where his biggest problem was how to ask a girl out. He hated what his life had become.

After picking up Johnny, they were well on their way to Chesterton's property. Johnny went over the plan again as they approached the wooded area by his home. They would park at the old park where Frankie had last weekend. Together they would approach Chesterton's home from the west side where Andrew would scale the wall around the perimeter and break into Chesterton's property. Johnny would then cut the security lines on the south side of the house and then wait for a few minutes before scaling the wall at an area where it was a little shorter.

"Turn here," Johnny said, pointing his finger toward a left turn. It was a dark area with no street lights, or much light at all. They quickly came upon an old parking area that marked the entrance to an overgrown trail. Under normal circumstances, Andrew would have been afraid to leave his car out here, but this was by no means a normal circumstance. They put their masks on and quickly exited the car.

The next few minutes seemed to pass very quickly. Andrew and Johnny ran through the woods as fast as they could. Leaves crunched under their feet as they passed through the trees. Andrew had a small bag on his side that was bouncing off his hip. He could feel himself sweat as they made the long run through the woods.

Johnny never once looked back to check on Andrew. He was focused. The past few days had been like a horror film to him. He longed to regain control over his life. He hated the idea of someone being a step ahead of him and messing with his friends and his girl. He felt confident he could catch Chesterton off guard tonight and at the very least threaten him. Possibly even use the gun on him if need be.

Andrew was starting to lose sight of Johnny when they made it to the wall. Johnny ducked down at the base of it. "Drew, give me about 20 minutes before you approach the house. That should give me plenty of time to find and cut the security lines. Stay in a shadowy spot until then."

"Ok."

"All right, man. Well, let's do this," Johnny said, bending over and cupping his hands. Andrew took the duffle bag off his shoulder and laid it on the ground. In one fluid motion, Andrew grabbed Johnny's shoulder and put his foot in his hands. Johnny quickly lifted and threw him over the wall. This time Andrew was able to grab the top and throw himself over, landing on his feet. Thankfully he was near a shadowy cover of the property where he could easily be concealed in the darkness of night. He looked down at his watch to check the time. His watch read 11:42 p.m. He would give Johnny the full twenty minutes to cut the line.

The minutes passed slowly as Andrew felt his heartbeat going in full stride. It was like he could almost hear it thumping in his chest. The house looked magnificent in the dead of night. The moonlight was reflecting off the swimming pool water along with a clear reflection of Chesterton's home. It was a glorious sight to behold.

As Andrew sat, he remembered the emotions that ran through him the last time he was in this situation. He remembered the fear and the regret. This time as he waited all he could think of was revenge. He thought about his brother lying in the hospital bed. He kept hearing the coughs of his mother in his ears. Chesterton had infected them and he was going to prove it. A part of him didn't care about Johnny's plan. He wanted evidence. He wanted something he could show to the police to prove to the town that Chesterton was a criminal. Chesterton would pay for this and pay deeply. Anger boiled over in him.

Andrew looked at his watch. Twenty minutes had gone by. He got up and walked along the edge of the wall, approaching the house. The house was dark and all the lights were off. Surely Chesterton was upstairs sleeping. This would be a complete surprise. Making it to a side glass door, Andrew was confident that Johnny had shut down Chesterton's security system. Andrew knocked out a small window pane and easily stuck his hand in and opened the door. He marveled at how easily and carelessly he broke into someone's home.

Once again the house looked wonderful, similar to how it had looked last time. Chesterton had obviously put everything back in order and there was no trace of the break-in from a week ago. Andrew was currently in the sunroom but quietly moved to the kitchen as the moonlight was shining through the windows.

Entering the kitchen, Andrew ducked beside the cabinets. He tried to quiet his breathing. He heard nothing; the house was silent. He slid himself across the tiled floor to the walk way of the living room. He stopped at the edge of the cabinets and peeked into the large living room. He saw everything was in order. The TV was back on the wall and it looked as if Chesterton had replaced the carpets. Most importantly, Andrew saw no one.

He quietly got up onto his feet and entered the living room. He was sure to check all the corners of the room as he didn't want any surprises. The room was wonderfully decorated and in any other circumstance Andrew would have loved to visit and check out the house.

He ducked to the side of the couch, looking to the far stairwell. Everything looked clear. Taking his phone out of his pocket, Andrew shot Johnny a quick text, letting him know he was about to ascend the stairwell. The plan at this point was that if everything seemed clear, Andrew would head up the stairs without caution, hopefully waking Chesterton and startling him. Johnny would then quickly enter through his bedroom window and confront him with his gun. It was a simple plan of quick distraction. It was beating Chesterton at his own game.

Andrew took a few deep breaths. Fear was welling up inside him. He hoped that Johnny's plan was foolproof. Putting the phone back into his pocket, he felt Chesterton's ring and card he had brought with him. His dad's words raced through his mind, *"If he gave these to you at one of his shows, then you need to somehow return these items to someone at the casino and then walk away. Do you hear me?"* His dad made it sound so easy. Andrew knew his dad wouldn't understand the pressures he was facing from Johnny and the others.

Trying to get his mind focused, Andrew counted to ten under his breath, "One, two, three…" he closed his eyes and clenched his fist. He would move fast. "Seven, eight, nine… here we go… ten." With that he jumped to his feet and ran through the living room and up the stairs. He felt as if each creak in the steps was an explosion. He didn't try to quiet them; he wanted to be sure that Johnny heard him coming. He felt like it was the longest run of his life when he finally made it upstairs. Trying to remember his bearings, he looked at all the closed doors and remembered Chesterton's bedroom was to the left of the steps. He raced over and grabbed the door handle. He felt light-headed, wondering what he would find on the other side of it. Twisting the handle, he pushed the door open and stepped inside.

It was dark. He quickly looked around the room and found it empty. He wasn't sure what to do. His fear began to increase greatly. His breathing picked up. Chesterton's bed was made as if it had never been slept in and everything seemed to be in order. Andrew stepped further in to have a look around.

He wondered where Chesterton was. Surely he thought that he would be in bed at this time. Looking all around the room he came face to face with the mirror again. Once again it caught him off guard seeing his reflection with his black mask on.

The dresser on which the mirror sat was empty. He remembered finding the ring there last time. He took a few steps closer. His reflection became bigger and bigger as he approached. He hated the look of himself in the mirror. It was the look of a common thief. Andrew began to shake at the sight of himself. He couldn't take it anymore. He took his mask off.

Looking at his face, he looked deep into his eyes. Thoughts of his family, his friends, along with Sophia's advice penetrated in his mind. His dad's words came to him again, *"If he gave these to you at one of his shows, then you need to somehow return these items to someone at the casino and then walk away. Do you hear me?"* Andrew thought about his dad's advice. He wasn't ready to abort Johnny's plan, but maybe this could still help the situation.

Andrew put his hand into his pocket and brought out the ring. He held it up in the mirror, looking at it one last time. He had thought about it a lot this past week. It had even haunted him at times. Not thinking about anything else, he quietly set it down back on the dresser in the same spot he had picked it up.

Starting to turn around he felt the barrel of a gun against the back of his head. He froze and slowly put his hands to the air. He couldn't believe he hadn't seen anyone in the room. "What are you doing?" the voice said in a whisper.

Andrew felt himself begin to shake. He froze, wondering who was behind him. "Answer me!" the voice said harshly.

"I was just returning the ring. I didn't do anything to it. I took it for a while and now… it's back."

The gun slowly dropped from the back of his head. A hand grabbed him on the shoulder and spun him around. Andrew could see it was Johnny, still with his black ski mask on. He looked angry. "No, Drew, you idiot! I mean what are you doing with your mask off?"

Andrew slowly looked back at the mirror and saw his reflection. He stuttered as he talked, "I... I don't know. It was like... I just had to see myself or something. Like I just... had to see my face."

Johnny shook his head in frustration, "Drew, you're crazy, man. You never take your mask off when you're in someone's place. Never!" He spoke intently, getting right in Andrew's face.

"Oh, I'm sorry. I don't know what... I was thinking."

Johnny slid the gun back up his sleeve, "Well, you got off easy this time, man. It looks like the house is empty. You were slow in getting in. I've already checked every room in the whole house."

"Well, what do you want to do, Johnny?"

He let out a deep breath, "I don't know, man. Maybe let's just take some of his electronics downstairs and get on our way. I don't feel like messing this place up again."

The boys left the bedroom and headed downstairs. Above all else, Andrew was thankful for an opportunity to return the ring. Hopefully this would only help their cause with Chesterton. Descending the steps, Johnny quickly scanned the room looking for anything that may be of value for pawning. He started giving out orders, "Drew, you start unhooking some of those speakers in the corner. I'm going to look in some of the storage closets and see if he has anything valuable in there."

Andrew didn't hear anything his friend said, for in the far corner he saw one of the kitchen chairs sitting in the doorway of the kitchen, and in the chair he saw a man.

Johnny could tell his friend was stunned, "Drew, what's the matter with you, man? Start looking around, we don't have much time."

Andrew just raised his index finger and pointed at the man. Johnny slowly turned to face a relaxed Chesterton sitting in the chair, smiling at the two boys. "Good evening, gentlemen," he said politely, rising to his feet. He was dressed in his stage tux, except without his hat. His brown hair was parted nicely as if he had just come from the stage.

Andrew and Johnny stood gazing at him not knowing what to do or say. The moment seemed surreal. They had spent every waking hour the past week thinking about this man and now he stood in front of them. A part of them wanted to run, but more importantly they wanted to talk.

He continued, taking a couple steps toward them, "You can take off your masks. I know who you are. I've been expecting you."

Chapter 17

⸻〰◦◦⟡◦◦⟡◦◦〰⸻

Aɴᴅʀᴇᴡ ɢʟᴀɴᴄᴇᴅ ᴀᴛ Jᴏʜɴɴʏ ᴡᴏɴᴅᴇʀɪɴɢ what his next move would be. He longed for Johnny to break the silence, to say something to show Chesterton that he was the one in control. Johnny stared intently at Chesterton, not taking his eyes off of him. He was calm, but it was clear he didn't know what to do. Johnny bent his head over slightly and removed his mask. He quickly ran his fingers through his hair.

"And why don't you do the same, Andrew," Chesterton said calmly. Andrew slowly followed suit and pulled his mask off. Everyone could clearly see that he was shaking in fear.

Johnny broke the silence, "What do you want with us?" he said with a snarl.

Chesterton quickly countered, "Perhaps I should ask you that. You are in *my* house."

"You know what I mean," Johnny said angrily, "You've been chasing us, terrorizing us this whole week."

"Me terrorizing you!" Chesterton laughed slightly, "I do believe you are the ones who first interrupted my show with your drunken antics, and then broke into my house. You think I'm the one who terrorized you?"

The room went silent again as Chesterton quietly walked to one of his couches and took a seat. He was relaxed, seemingly not worried about anything. He continued, "I believe that you have something of mine... something small, but very important."

Johnny took a couple steps closer, "Look man, I saw Drew upstairs returning your stupid ring. Stealing that little thing is no reason for you to follow us and mess with our lives. Do you know what you did to my girl?"

Chesterton smiled, "Angela, you mean? Look, Johnny Platt," he said condescendingly, "you had to know I was serious. You can't just take things from a magician and not expect to reap the consequences of what you sow."

Johnny took another step closer, "You've got your ring, man, now leave us alone!" he said, shouting.

Chesterton quickly stood up, "Johnny, you keep forgetting you are in my house. And besides, the ring is not what I'm looking for." As if by instinct, Andrew reached his hand into his pocket and grabbed a hold of the silver plated card. He held it tightly.

Johnny continued, "Listen, man, we took some of your tricks but you can have them back, we didn't..."

Chesterton broke out into a full fledged laugh, "You really think I would be that stupid as to leave the blueprints of my best tricks lying around? You can keep those old things, plus parts of them are written in code. You wouldn't be able to figure them out anyway." Chesterton turned to face a mirror on his wall, "You stole *a part* of my tricks. A valuable item that I want back."

Andrew could see the gun slide down Johnny's wrist. He knew this was about to get ugly. Johnny continued to shout, "Listen man, I don't know what you're talking about. You drop off and stop messing with my girl and my school or I'm gonna…"

"Hold up," Andrew said, putting his hands up. Both sets of eyes turned to fix on him. "Is this what you want?" He said, taking the silver plated card out of his pocket. Andrew held it up, showing its beautiful silver plated design. He then flipped it over, showing the Ace of Hearts.

Chesterton smiled, and spoke pleasantly, "Yes, that is what I'm looking for."

Andrew nervously walked in between Johnny and Chesterton and set the card on a small coffee table. "Thank you, my boy," Chesterton said, giving Andrew a small wink.

"Fine, are we even now?" Johnny said harshly.

The next few seconds seemed like minutes as Chesterton quietly walked over to the table and picked up the card. He held it up in the little bit of light coming in through the windows. He admired it, the beauty of its design. One could easily see that he was happy to have it back. Andrew and Johnny both waited for Chesterton's reply. He seemed to be in no hurry. It almost seemed like he had forgotten that Andrew and Johnny were still in the room. He turned around and started walking back toward the kitchen.

Johnny yelled out again in frustration, "Chesterton, answer me! Are we done? Is this the end of it?"

With that Chesterton stopped and turned around; his smile was unforgettable. It was an image Andrew would never forget. It was evil. He spoke very articulately, "Well, we wouldn't want the fun to stop now, would we? I still have many more plans for you guys. I am only beginning."

Johnny quickly brought the gun up and pointed it toward Chesterton. Andrew could see Johnny was sweating profusely. He spoke through gritted teeth, "Listen man, I don't know what you're up to, but you leave us alone and stay away!"

Chesterton was calm, "Johnny, you're not really going to shoot me. I know you well enough to know you don't have the courage."

He began to shake, "Look here, man, I will kill you. You hear me! I will pull this trigger and lay you out cold. I don't care."

Andrew felt lightheaded. It was all happening so fast. He didn't know who he feared more at this point, Johnny or Chesterton. He quickly tried to think of a way to diffuse the situation. Andrew didn't know where this was going to lead, but he knew that he didn't want to be a part of it.

He saw that Chesterton was about to speak when he quickly interrupted, "Listen! Johnny, put the gun down, man."

"Shut up, Drew!"

Andrew was not going to be deterred. He continued, "Ok, Ok... umm... Mr. Chesterton, please, I beg of you, please just leave us alone. We'll repay anything we've damaged, and we'll walk away. Let's just end this."

"Andrew, like I said to Johnny, this is too much fun, and I've already got more plans in place. You won't be able to hide," Chesterton answered.

"Drew, I said shut up!" Johnny shouted as loud as he could.

Andrew got down low, on his knees as he continued, "Ok, shh... umm... ok... Mr. Chesterton, please I ask of you, actually more than that, I beg of you," Andrew put his hands up in a defenseless position. He was trembling, "Please, just stay away from my family. They can't take it. I can't see them like this."

Andrew's voice began to crack as he spoke, "They're all I've got. You can't take them from me. I need them, please."

Chesterton seemed to be taken aback by Andrew's comments. He squinted his eyes as he looked at Andrew. There was obvious confusion on his face. Reaching up, he gently tugged the collar of his tuxedo. He looked as if he was choosing his words carefully. He smiled a little, "You give me too much credit, Andrew. Sure, I struck Frankie's family, but after watching you, I'm not sure how much you love them anyway. I wasn't sure it would be worth my time to strike your family."

Andrew was confused, "What? What are you talking about? My brother's in the hospital with an infection that's about to kill him." Andrew's voice was rising, "Don't say you know nothing about this."

"Listen Andrew, like I said… I didn't touch your family."

Andrew quickly got off his knees, "You liar. You hurt my brother and now you've made my mom sick too!"

Chesterton shook his head, "Andrew, you're starting to annoy me. I know who your father is… and I mean, I know who he really is. I have not nor am I going to mess with your family. If you're here to settle some score concerning them, you are in the wrong place. I suggest you get out of here as quickly as you can and let me and your friend, Johnny, sort out our differences."

Andrew couldn't believe what he just heard. Though he didn't fully trust Chesterton, he knew in his heart of hearts that Chesterton was telling the truth. He had no part in his family's sicknesses, particularly with Elliot's infection. He thought back to last week when he broke his brother's nose, solely out of anger for wrecking his car. Andrew hurt at the thought that he had put his brother through this. Elliot may die because of his actions, not Chesterton's. All of it was truly his fault. A small part of him wanted to challenge Chesterton, but he knew it would be in vain. He felt sick.

Andrew would have stayed there in deep thought, except for the fact that Johnny snapped him out of it. "Drew, you heard him! Get out of here! Right now, this is between me and this idiot. We've got to finish it!"

Chesterton shook his head and spoke slowly, "Johnny, Johnny, we're not going to finish anything tonight. This night is going to end with you running away like a scared little girl."

"Don't say I won't do it, man. Don't say I won't do it."

Andrew didn't want to wait around and see what would happen next. He turned around and faced the front door. He quickly ran towards it. Trembling, he unlocked the deadbolt and flung the door open. He stepped outside and ran down the steps and onto the front walkway. He was breathing heavily with fear, wondering exactly what he should do next. Andrew quietly whispered a prayer under his breath, "Help me, God. Please, get me out of this. I need you now. Please help me."

Reaching the front gate, he easily pulled down the manual release, swinging open one of the doors. He stepped out. Taking a few steps he felt relief, freedom. His breathing began to slow slightly. The fear started to subside.

He was about ten paces from the gate, almost to the road, when he heard a sound he would never forget… a loud gunshot coming from Chesterton's home!

Chesterton lay on the floor. Blood was coming from his left ribs. He pressed the spot tightly where the bullet penetrated. He was moaning in pain. Johnny walked over to where he was lying. The gun was still in his hand; he was shaking. Tears began to flow from his eyes.

"I told you I would do it, man. I told you," he said through his tears.

Chesterton breathed deeply. He put his head up slightly and looked at Johnny, "Don't think this is going to save you." His voice was faint, "I'm still coming after you, your girl, and then your family. Nothing can save you, Johnny Platt. I've got you. You're mine." Chesterton laughed under his breath.

Johnny closed his eyes. The tears were flowing like a fountain. He put his hands over his eyes and squeezed the trigger again, hitting Chesterton squarely in the stomach. He heard Chesterton groan with pain. Squeezing the trigger again he let out another shot, this time in his right ribs.

Not wanting to see what he had done, Johnny turned and took a few steps toward the front door. His strength had left him. His legs felt like they weighed a hundred pounds each. Slowly making his way to the door, he collapsed in the doorway and pulled himself outside.

He couldn't believe he'd killed a man. He was the king of pranks and mischief but he never thought it would lead him to this. With the power and popularity he'd had the last few years, he felt untouchable. Johnny had always been a step ahead of everyone, including the school administration. He'd become addicted to the power he had accumulated and he realized that he couldn't live without being in control. Even for just a week it was unbearable, and now it had led him to kill a man. He didn't know how he would ever live with himself.

He was in a fetal position, crying on Chesterton's porch when he heard the sirens pull up. Quickly getting up and gathering himself, he saw that four or five Waterloo police cars had arrived. Strangely, Johnny had not thought of the police. With the last break in, Chesterton had worked hard at keeping them away and now he didn't even consider the possibility that they might be called. He was dumbfounded at himself for not considering this.

A couple officers filed out of each car and pointed their guns at Johnny. "Hands in the air!" they yelled. Johnny obeyed.

It all happened so fast. A couple cops were quickly on Johnny, gathering his gun and putting him in cuffs. A few others were going into Chesterton's home. He heard one on the police radio say that a bystander had heard shots fired and called it in.

The scene was chaos, but what Johnny would remember most of all would be looking over to the spot where Chesterton laid and realizing that he was gone.

Andrew had left Chesterton's property in a hurry and had quickly gotten back to his car. He had run along the edge of the woods and hadn't looked back. He didn't want any part of Chesterton's games anymore. He knew that if he'd stayed at the house he would be further roped into Chesterton's web of deception and amusement. He had to break free.

He knew the one place he wanted to go… to the hospital. There was no other place he wanted to be than with his family. They needed him now. Andrew drove straight to the hospital, giving no thought of turning around and seeing what happened back at Chesterton's home. He was determined to make his family his first priority.

He pulled into the hospital parking lot and swiftly changed out of his black shirt. He got out of his car, slamming the door hard. He carried his black shirt and ski mask with him. As he ran toward the visitor entrance, he quickly stuffed them into a nearby trash can. He then continued on toward the entrance. He couldn't get inside fast enough.

Andrew casually walked past the front desk receptionist, straight up to his brother's room. The hospital was quiet and he was able to make it to Elliot's room without speaking to anybody. Standing in front of the door, he took a deep breath. He knew what he had to do. The tears started to swell in his eyes as he slowly opened the door.

His parents were still by Elliot's side. Both were wide awake and looking over their younger son. They turned to face Andrew. His mom quickly stood up. She was completely caught off guard to see him. "Andrew, what are you doing here?" she asked quietly.

Andrew wondered what to say in that moment, but the words didn't come to him. He stood in the doorway completely quiet and the tears began to fall. He put his hand over his eyes, trying to hide the tears. It was all in vain as they started to flow freely.

"Andrew?" his mom quickly ran to embrace him. Holding her tightly, he buried his head into her shoulder. This was exactly where he wanted to be. His dad followed suit, getting up from his chair. He walked over and put his big burly arms around his wife and son.

They stood in silence holding each other as the minutes passed by. Eventually, Andrew spoke through his tears, "I just had to see him. I just... (sniff) wanted him to know that I love him."

His mom smiled at him. Andrew could see tears in her eyes. "Shh... it's all right, Son," she said patiently. "Everything's going to be all right. He knows you love him."

Pulling back, Andrew spoke softly to his parents, "Is it all right if I have a few more minutes with him alone? I just feel like I need to talk to him. There's something I need to say."

Diane Stevenson looked confused at her son's request. This was truly not like Andrew. She was thinking about what to ask next when her husband broke the silence, "Sure, Son, that'll be all right. If you feel like you need to talk with him then I think that will be most appropriate." His mom gave him one more tight squeeze before calmly walking over to grab her purse and then heading out the door.

His father was about to leave when his eyes met his son's. He gave Andrew a small wink as he stepped out. Andrew felt that his father knew what he was about to do. His father was a man of mystery at times and he always seemed to be a step ahead of him.

Andrew slowly walked over to where his brother lay. He was still fast asleep. He was heavily medicated and appeared to be in a deep sleep. Andrew took off his glasses and laid them on a nearby tray. The tears were still coming, and he knew they wouldn't be stopping anytime soon.

He grabbed his brother's hand and held it tightly with both of his own hands. He felt cold. Andrew bent over and held Elliot's hand close to his forehead. The tears came on strong once again. Something about the touch of his hand made him realize how much he loved his brother. Andrew felt guilty for putting him here. It made him sick, thinking about breaking his brother's nose. It was a stupid car with a dent. How could he have done this? People are more important than things.

He looked up intently at his brother and spoke softly through his tears, "Elliot, I'm so sorry. I'm sorry for everything; for hitting you, for breaking your nose, for not being here for you." He quickly wiped his tears as he continued, "I'm sorry for being such a lousy brother... please forgive me."

Elliot started to stir slightly in his bed. He didn't wake up, but Andrew felt a gentle squeeze of his hand. Bending over again, he held it close to his forehead. He whispered a prayer, "God, forgive me. I don't know what I've done, or what I'm doing. Help me! I can't do this life alone. Help me to make things right. I'm just... so sorry... so sorry." That was all Andrew was able to say. The tears were coming on too strong. He was broken.

Chapter 18

CHARLES CHESTERTON SAT COMFORTABLY BACKSTAGE in his office, his feet resting comfortably on his desk. Six months had passed since he had been shot by Johnny. So much had happened since that night. He held the Ace of Hearts in his hand. He admired it. It had become a symbol of power to him. At the moment it was bringing him deep satisfaction. He almost wondered if he should have it framed.

He thought about the trial that had just ended a few days ago, *the State of Iowa vs. Johnny Platt*. It truly was one to remember. It was a case that had baffled the judge, the lawyers, as well as spectators. All who were involved, along with those who followed the case via the local news, were truly mystified by it.

During the trial Johnny had come clean, telling the whole story about how he had interrupted Chesterton's show, broken into his home, and then shot him. Chesterton denied a lot of Johnny's testimony including being shot. The court room became a confusing scene as the defense was claiming it did shoot Chesterton, whereas Chesterton, speaking as a witness for the prosecution, claimed he was never shot. The local press, along with a few national news organizations, ate it up. The story was fascinating to many legal minds.

The jury eventually sided more with the prosecution, being very sympathetic with Chesterton. Johnny was charged with breaking and entering, as well as attempted assault. He was sentenced to five years in prison. With good behavior he hoped to be out in less than three.

Chesterton, on the other hand, gained massive popularity through the case. Every show, every night was selling out a few weeks ahead of time. He was in high demand for news and talk shows everywhere. He put Waterloo, Iowa on the map. Many travel magazines and brochures started marketing Waterloo as the home of Charles Chesterton.

More than all of this, Chesterton was looked at as a man of mystery and wonder. The mysterious case involving Johnny Platt elevated the perception of him as something more than a magician. He was a wonder worker, a man to be feared, not just on the stage, but also in life. People adored him, but also lived in fear of him both as a performer and as a man.

Grabbing his ribs, he thought back to the day he was shot. It took him a few months to heal from the couple of cracked ribs he sustained. The shots hurt, but thankfully his extra strength bullet proof vest had held up, and even at a close range no real damage had occurred. It was amazing the type of trick one could do with a thick bullet proof vest and a few blood capsules. He chuckled at the thought of it.

On the night of the shooting, Chesterton was actually disappointed the police had been called. A newly engaged couple was out for a late night stroll, not far from Chesterton's property when they heard shots fired. They quickly called the police, who were not far from the area. Seeing the police pull in, Chesterton quickly got up, ran upstairs, and hid in his closet. He told the police he was extremely frightened by the intruder who was firing shots.

In reality, Chesterton had an elaborate scheme laid out. He was hoping Johnny would quietly leave the premises, thinking he had killed him. Chesterton could then further terrorize him as one that came back from the dead. The plan seemed ingenious. He was mildly disappointed it had not come to full fruition.

Even still he got what he wanted. People everywhere were left in fearful wonder of him. His whole life felt like one grand magic trick. He truly was the Ace of Hearts. He could captivate anyone's soul and leave them in terror and wonder. The card itself wasn't vital to any stage performance, but he was glad the boys found it on the night of the break-in. The card had actually become a source of misdirection for him. He wanted them to think it was the reason for his retaliation.

He thought back to that day in his office in Reno when he was beginning to feel like he was in a cage, just performing tricks like some sort of circus animal. That was not what he wanted to be… he wanted to be the Ace of Hearts. Even if it was just a few people, he wanted to leave them in fearful wonder. He wanted to tame a person's intellect, will, and emotions with his tricks.

All of this had been accomplished with the four college boys. He had their hearts on a leash. They feared him, thought about him, and wondered how he performed his tricks. It was exactly what he wanted. He had tamed four souls, and though presently some were slipping out of his hands, it brought him great joy that at one point they were his.

Chesterton put the card down and laughed quietly. In his heart was something was very dark. Jerry Stevenson was right, Chesterton was truly evil.

Dax was in a gas station somewhere in the middle of Wyoming. The past six months he had been traveling through the Dakotas, trying to hide. He lived out of his car and took whatever odd jobs he could find. As of the past couple weeks, he was working for a cattle farmer who was desperately looking for help.

This station was known for having the cheapest beer in town. Dax quickly grabbed a case of Budweiser and took it to the counter. He was dirty from a hard day's work and was craving some alcohol. He was drinking more these days; anxiety was getting to him with each passing week.

Setting the beer up on the counter, he nodded slightly at the young cashier. "How ya' doing?" he said casually.

"Doin' fine, thank you," the cashier responded. He was dressed like a true Wyoming cowboy, hat and all. "Did you get any gas?"

"No, just the beer."

"All right, well your total comes to $23.53," he said, reaching out his hand.

Dax quickly pulled out his wallet and gave the cashier the money in cash. He had gotten into the habit of not using a credit card so he couldn't be tracked. He wanted to completely disappear.

"Thank you very much," the cashier responded. Dax quickly grabbed the beer and headed out to the door. He was looking forward to finding a quiet spot and drinking himself to sleep.

He was just about to walk out the door, when the cashier stopped him. "Oh, hold up here now... one more thing."

Dax turned to face the man, who was grabbing something from under the counter. "Yes?"

"Is your name... uh ... Dax?" he asked.

Dax stood there in silence for a second, wondering about the meaning of this. He finally responded, "Yes, that's me."

"Well, this came to me a couple hours ago. I was told to deliver it to you," the cashier said, holding out a small envelope in his hands with Dax's name on the front.

Dax quickly walked over and grabbed it from the man's hand. He continued, "I'm not sure how they knew you were goin' to come by, but nonetheless they said you would, and..."

Dax didn't let the man finish. He was already out the door and halfway to his car. This was standard procedure every couple weeks. He received a card, either hand delivered or in the mail. They always seemed to find him.

He quickly got into his car and tore open the envelope. It was, of course, from Chesterton. It simply read,

Hello Lanky,

How's Wyoming? I hope they aren't working you too hard on the farm. Be assured that wherever you go or whatever you do, I'll be watching over you. You can never escape. I will always be here.

See you soon,
Charles Chesterton

Dax began to shake with fear, wondering how Chesterton found him. He looked all around, wondering if Chesterton could see him. He feared he was close. He started to sweat. He had felt confident that Chesterton wouldn't find him here in the middle of Wyoming. He had hoped that this time he had lost him. Of course, as always, Dax was wrong.

He thought about what he was going to do next. His first step would be to sell his car right away and then relocate to the Pacific Northwest, possibly even into Canada. Maybe if he was in a different country Chesterton would never find him. He didn't care where he had to go. He just knew that he had to keep running.

Fresh tears started to flow from his eyes as he pulled out of the parking lot.

Frankie was in his first weeks of his community service at the Cedar Falls Rescue Mission, located west of Waterloo. Thankfully, he received very little prison time because of the assault. The judge had ordered him to countless hours of community service along with psychiatric counseling.

Currently he was loading boxes of clothing donations into a storage unit. Even in the cool October air, sweat was pouring down his face. It was hard work, but he didn't mind. The mission stood for a good cause, and through their counsel and love he had found real hope.

His family had been greatly disappointed with him because of the assault, but through it they were able to talk through many issues that had been plaguing Frankie for years. He constantly lived with the idea that he had never measured up to the success and stability of his brothers and sister. He also felt like he was a failure to his mom and dad.

He ended up confessing to his family that the assault was an attempt to get revenge on the man who infected their mother. They were shocked to hear this, but in the end they didn't seem to care about the criminal as much as they cared for Frankie. They hated seeing him in prison, and the last thing they wanted for him was to feel like he had to take justice into his own hands. They assured him that he was accepted just because he was part of their family, not because of anything he did.

"Frankie," his supervisor interrupted him in his work.

He quickly put down the box he was holding and wiped his forehead, "Yes?"

"This just came for you," he said, handing him a small envelope with his name on the front.

"Thank you," he returned. He knew exactly what it was. He had received one every couple of weeks for the last few months. It was from Chesterton: a letter to pester him, to terrify him, to stir him up.

He stood looking at it for a minute, focusing on his name written on the front. He was tempted to open it. A part of him wanted to see what was written, and to see how much Chesterton knew of his current life. He was tempted, but in the end Frankie did what he always did with the letters… threw them right in the trash. He didn't want anything to do with Chesterton or his games anymore. He was breaking free and he never wanted to go back. His mother was a hundred percent healed, and he was now working his way back into society.

He was so thankful for this mission, specifically the chaplain, for helping him break the cycle of fear and doubt that had haunted his life for so long. His family loved and accepted him and that was enough for him. He didn't need Johnny Platt or Charles Chesterton in his life.

Johnny was bench pressing out in the prison yard. This was his daily routine. He had gained a lot of muscle mass since being in prison. All of the guys knew who he was and he had quickly gained credibility among the other inmates. He was a leader among them, and even in prison he got what he wanted.

He wiped his forehead as he turned to face his spotter. "Let's do one more. I'm feeling good today."

"Whatever you say, boss," his spotter responded.

Normally Johnny struggled a little on his last set, but not today. The mundane routine of prison was starting to get to him. He was ready to be out and getting out meant taking another strike at Chesterton. With every flex of his bicep he thought about what his next move would be. It was already planned out. As soon as he got out, he would strike before Chesterton could realize what was happening.

Finishing out the set, his spotter helped him set the bar back on the rack. He grabbed his towel and wiped his forehead. He had worked hard this morning. Putting on his faded green prison shirt, he began at the bottom buttoning it up. He was almost at the top when a prison guard interrupted him, "Johnny Platt?"

"Yes," he said, irritated.

"This came for you today. The person who delivered it said it was urgent." The guard held out a small envelope with Johnny's name written on the front. Johnny sat staring at it for a few seconds before grabbing it. He knew exactly what it was; each month he had received a new one.

Even though he was using a pseudonym, Johnny knew it was a letter from Chesterton. In an earlier letter Chesterton had implied that he would be using his uncle's name, so that no one could trace the letters back to him. Either way, Johnny didn't care whose name was signed to the letter. He was never going to the police. He was determined to settle this on his own. Johnny gently tore the seal on the back and opened it. As always, not much was written. This time it said,

Johnny,

I hope your day is going well and you're enjoying your little cage. It's no fun, is it? I've heard that you are trying to bulk up. Good for you! I would like to make it a fair fight when you get out. Keep trying young man, and I look forward to seeing you soon.

Best wishes,
Alex Wellington

He could feel the anger rising up inside. He tore the letter into many pieces. Throwing them on the ground, he began stomping on them like a mad man. His boot pressed each piece deep into the dirt. Revenge consumed him. He could think of nothing else but Chesterton. Revenge truly was his cage, not the prison bars.

Johnny quickly stood to his feet and found his spotter, who was casually walking away. He yelled out, "Hey kid, get back over here," he said harshly, "I'm going to hit another set today."

Andrew parallel parked in front of Sophia's house. He had sold his silver Mustang and was now driving a small used Ford Focus. There were too many bad memories with the Mustang. Time had passed since he'd last hung out with Sophia, and they had plans to go to dinner and then catch a movie. This time Andrew was going to stay true to his word. He wanted to do things right.

The past six months had been hard. He failed most of his classes in the spring semester because of the time he missed while dealing with Chesterton. He had always been a good student and his mother was quite upset with him. His father never asked about his grades; he knew that his son had been messing with Charles Chesterton.

Over the summer and into the fall semester Andrew dealt with a lot of his internal strife. He struggled with the idea of perfection and not measuring up. The incident with his brother led him to think more about forgiveness. He longed for forgiveness to be granted to him for what he did. Conviction overcame him and his confession in the hospital was the first step toward a long road of forgiveness.

Thankfully, Andrew's brother, Elliot, fully recovered from his sickness. The doctors were able to get his medicine under control a few days after Andrew's apology, and from there it was a quick upward journey toward good health. Elliot easily accepted his brother's apology and their relationship was better than it had ever been.

Through it all, Andrew radically changed. He started attending church and really trying to listen to the sermons. He wholeheartedly embraced the concepts of love and forgiveness, and they completely changed his personality. Sophia noticed this change in Andrew and invited him to hang with her today. They had become better friends through it all.

Opening the door to his car, he was about to get out when he noticed a small envelope on the passenger seat. He picked it up, reading his name on the front. He knew what it was. Every couple of weeks he expected to receive a note from Chesterton. He found them at random spots either at school, in his car, or even around town. He wasn't sure how they were delivered.

At first he was frightened by how much Chesterton was watching him, but he had become immune to it over time. His dad knew about the cards and encouraged him to not let it bother him. He kept telling his son that more than anything Chesterton wanted his heart, to manipulate it, to hold it in his hand, and to own it. The warning rang true in his head. Andrew put the card under his seat. He didn't want Sophia to see it. He figured he'd open it later, just in case there was something he needed to know.

Getting out of his car, his mind quickly reverted back to the task at hand. He took his glasses off and wiped the lenses against his shirt. Brushing his hair to the side, he walked up to Sophia's front door. Before he could knock, the door swung open and there was Sophia smiling brightly. She was dressed casually. Her beautiful blonde hair was had grown long, close to her waist. She looked gorgeous.

"H… Hey," Andrew said nervously.

"Hey Andrew, you ready to go?" she said, putting on a pair of sunglasses.

"Sure, I mean… if you're r… r… ready to go that is," he said, stuttering.

"Absolutely!" she said, walking out the door and pulling it shut. "Hopefully we *are* going to a movie this time," she said, smiling at Andrew.

"Oh, yes… yes, sure," he said stumbling over his words, "just going out to dinner and then seeing a movie. Not a date, no surprises, or anything like that. Just a simple time together as friends."

Sophia laughed a little under her breath, amused at how nervous Andrew was. She brushed her hair out of her eyes. She thought for a moment before speaking up, "Well, I guess… this time you can call it a date," she said smiling. She took a few paces toward his car before stopping and facing him. The smile disappeared from her face, and her expression became serious, "But Andrew Stevenson," she said emphatically, "you'd better not try to kiss me!"

Epilogue

It was a very dark day in Waterloo. Rain had been pouring down for much of the day. Angela Rodriguez walked toward the casino with her arm around the bicep of an Eastern Iowa football player. At the moment he was her new man, and she had big plans for him. He was going to become another victim of Charles Chesterton. It was already planned out, and surely it would not fail. Everything was coming together so beautifully.

She thought back to that fateful day a couple of years ago, when Charles called her into his office with ideas for his new "trick." At the time she had been operating more as his manager, and both of them had become bored of the magic industry as it had been playing out in Reno. He told her of a plan to recapture the wonder of magic, not with illusions, but with fear. He would learn how to tame the hearts of people, not just during a performance, but every waking hour of their lives. It was truly diabolical, but it was what he wanted.

Angela, at first, was wary of his plan, but he promised to compensate her heavily for her efforts. She would also have to take part in the tricks, and switch roles from his manager to his assistant. She would be a vital part of the act, and as any magician knows, "A beautiful woman in a magic show is one of the best distractions a magician can have." She was the biggest distraction in the life of these college kids.

Helping Chesterton tame the boys' hearts was an easy task. She had encouraged them to go to the show, and then being sure they consumed enough alcohol to make them "rowdy," she easily implanted the lipstick and handkerchief in Johnny's pocket without him knowing. Thankfully, Johnny and Dax caused enough problems during the show to make Chesterton call them out. All he had to do was botch one simple trick. Chesterton hated messing up his trick, but it was well worth it.

Though Johnny thought he had her wrapped around his finger, in actuality Angela was provoking him with every move. She was a good actress, and thankfully, Johnny's temper and competitive spirit made him easy to provoke. It was almost too easy. She was in constant communication with Chesterton and even helped him get his house in order before the boys broke in. They were definitely a team.

Angela and her new man entered the auditorium and took their seats toward the front, nearly the same seats she had occupied with Johnny. She smiled at her new man as she put her head on his shoulder and slipped a couple embarrassing photos into his pocket. She loved "performing" with Chesterton.

The lights went dim as Chesterton came onto the stage. Everyone applauded as he began,

"Every magician has a repertoire of tricks that he regularly performs. These are his favorites and he does not stray from them. You will see many of these tonight. BUT! A magician often becomes complacent and disinterested in his own tricks. He must look for new ways to entertain, not just his audience, but also himself. So without further ado, let us begin, shall we?"

Angela loved that speech… she helped him write it.

"Sin will take you further than you want to
go, keep you longer than you want to stay, and
cost you more than you want to pay."
- Unknown

"The thief comes only to steal and kill and destroy. I
came that they may have life and have it abundantly."
- Jesus (John 10:10)

About the author

———⁓∿∘◦⊙⊰⊙⊀◦∘∿⁓———

Tony Myers is a high school youth pastor and hospice chaplain. He enjoys looking for creative ways and illustrations to communicate truth. He and his wife, Charity, have three kids and currently live in Waterloo, Iowa. Visit his website at www.tonymyers.net or follow him on Twitter @tony1myers.

Also, check out Tony Myers' first book *Singleton*, published by Westbow Press. Available at most online book retailers.

"*Singleton* engages your heart, soul, and mind. With tension between its characters and mysteries regarding the plot, this book is not easy to put down! Just when you think Jack's situation can't get any worse, it does. The father/daughter bond he shares with Olivia and his deteriorating marriage string the reader along until the very end. Amid unanswered questions and a wide range of emotions, fight the urge to read ahead! The ending of this book makes an impression that will be difficult to forget."

- Rachel Banasky

"As someone with a lifelong interest in magic who has been fooling people as long as I remember, I love the chance to be fooled myself. As I read *Singleton* I was baffled. The first few pages of the book caught my attention just like the opening trick of a good magic show. From there I was kept in suspense as the mystery unfolded. Just when I thought it was impossible to tie together all the strange things which were occurring, Myers performs his best trick. In the last few pages of the book he brings the mystery to a satisfying yet shocking conclusion. Like a good magic show *Singleton* leaves you wanting more. Fortunately Myers has another book up his sleeve. If you are like me and enjoy a good mystery, then you may want to consider *Stealing the Magic* for yourself. If *Singleton* is any indication, it is bound to entertain and keep you in suspense."

- John Neely, Magician